ABHORRENT ACCORDS

JOHN BALTISBERGER

This book is dedicated to Dr. Freidberg and Dr. Meeneghan and their teams who kept me alive through my fight with and helped me beat cancer.

"Be wary of authorities who befriend a person for their own purposes. They appear loving when it is beneficial to them, but do not stand by the other person in his time of distress"
—Rabban Gamliel, Avot 2:3

BOUND TO BE REPEATED

HISTORY IS USUALLY written by the victor; instead, we're writing it. There are no victors here. There are plenty of heroes and villains, sure. But in the end, for there to be a victor, someone has to claim victory. The war has to have a finale. The battle has to be won. The nightmare has to end. There is no end to the Abhorrent nightmare. It's a world we crafted with our own blood-stained hands; some would argue that it's the world we deserve.

"We." I use that word lightly; humanity is a fractured thing. It always has been, of course, since Cain brained Abel with a jagged rock in the fields for serving the same god in different ways. The first holy war in which the name of the divine was invoked to evoke murderous rage. This was a holy war. It didn't have to be; it shouldn't have been. Humanity should have come together to fight. Instead, greed prevailed, as it always does, and the Abhorrence and everything that came with it was allowed to sweep the world in its terrible pink mist.

One day, if humanity does survive, maybe we can learn from this; we can take a good hard look at ourselves and the world that now exists and know how to set aside petty dalliances and perverse narcissism. Know that it is literally the only way we can survive. I doubt it, though. Throughout all of human history, it has echoed, bouncing off the walls of time to collide against us again and again. Our greed knows no bounds, and we would rather watch the world burn than help someone, no matter how easy it would be to do so.

Some people will disagree with me, of course. They'll say we won the war, that humanity triumphed, that my nihilistic views and words cheapen the miles of gore and shredded flesh that stretches across the land and chokes the rivers and tributaries of the world. I try not to judge them; people need their optimism, their hope. I wouldn't want to take that from them. But as I look across the devastated landscape—cities torn apart and the mass graves and facilities that still work around the clock to cremate the dead—towards the isolated places where we know there are still nests of the afflicted breeding, I have to question what they could possibly mean by victory.

The nightmare isn't over; I doubt it ever will be. Even if we had been able to wipe the afflicted from the face of the planet, we will always have to look over our shoulder, wondering when the next Abhorrent Event might happen. And it will happen again. I doubt there are even enough of us left to deal with it when it does.

The world was forever changed when the Abhorrent crawled out of whatever caves under the Rio Grande River gave birth to it. But it wasn't a sudden change. The Abhorrence, as it's been called, the effects of the tainted opiates, had already begun to pop up, isolated incidents that were covered up or explained away. Sometimes I wonder if we had been aware, if we had noticed the signs, if we could have done anything differently.

The truth—I would be willing to put money on—is that the only difference it would have made is how quickly people would have tried to weaponize it. History is written by the victor, and despite the words I am committing

JOHN BALTISBERGER

to page here, we, humanity that is,
most certainly lost.

Alexander Fienkolt
University of Texas, Archivist

PART I:

EMERGENCE

THE STATE OF THE PRE-EMERGENCE WORLD

BEFORE THE EMERGENCE, or the Abhorrence, whatever you want to call it, humanity was complacent in the not-so-slow decline of the world. Identity politics were being used across the board to politicize everything from disease and natural disasters to mass shootings with clear cut motives. Even the most rational of us were blinded by it. How could we find common ground with people who believed the most benign things were terrible conspiracies while sitting in happy silence as corrupt criminals openly broke the law as elected officials? I remember during Hurricane Hillary in the early 2020s, one newscaster blamed the democratic president opening the borders for the hurricane crossing from Mexico to America.

Sure, we, all of us, were angry, but everyone felt powerless. We knew the world was becoming more inhospitable and more hostile every day. But we thought it would either get better or it would stabilize and would be our new reality.

The Abhorrence happened too quickly, so suddenly that there was no time for talking heads. In fact, a huge number of the American leaderships quickly fell to the Abhorrence themselves, emerging from their homes and offices as monsters.

But that's only what we could see. How many changes happened in the back streets and alleyways? How many homeless or dispossessed changed and hid, taking victims from the shadows before the mass emergence of the afflicted? We will probably never have those answers; they probably only matter in helping us foresee new events.

But what we do know is that the first official report of an incident that has survived came from a Mexican police officer, Frederico Sanchez, mere hours before the Emergence began in earnest.

Alexander Fienkolt
University of Texas, Archivist

THE FIRST RECORDED INCIDENT
FREDERICO SANCHEZ

I.

RICO WASN'T EXPECTING it to be so gross. Being a federal officer on the border, he had seen plenty of terrible things. Between the cruelty of the Americans and the viciousness of the Cartels, he had always known that this place was hell—the liminal nightmare between the worst of American bigotry and the greed of the drug dealers.

So when he was called to investigate a body washed up on the shore of the Rio Grande, he, along with his fellow officers, all acted like it wasn't a big deal. That was part of their MO, though; no one wanted to admit that stuff freaked them out, they didn't want anyone to think they were pussies. So they gathered their gear, hopped in the truck, and headed north to the river banks. The group of men blustered and talked about how the fucking cartels needed to be stopped, but it was lip service, right?

"No, man, put me in a room with one of those motherfuckers," Beto Costa was saying. "I'll get them talking in no time." He pulled out his handgun, a chrome plated .45 he had lifted from evidence. It was a gangster's gun, a showpiece. He stroked it lovingly, as if it were his cock and he was trying to show a new girlfriend how big it could get.

"Talking about what?" Miguel Villa asked.

"Yeah, and what would you do?" Manni Alfonso followed up.

"Shit, you know, I'd fucking put the fear of Beto into

them, get them to give up their boss, get some real intel and fuck them up."

"So," Rico said, "you think that the reason we don't arrest Don Hernandez is because we don't know who he is? Where he is?"

All four men laughed; you could practically see Hernandez's mansion, La Tierra Abundante, from space.

"Still, man, get the layout, guard rotations, figure that out, slip in-slip out," Beto said, trying to save face.

"What are you, the fucking Mexican James Bond? Jaime Bondito?" Miguel barked.

"Man, fuck your mom, pussy," Beto muttered, his face red.

"Hey, no, man, don't get all pissy just because Miguel doesn't have the balls to be a hero," Rico said, trying to soothe Beto's ego.

"It's not that I don't have the balls," Miguel said. "It's that I want to keep them!"

None of them actually thought the cartels could be stopped. None of them wanted to do anything to get in their way. They didn't want to be targets; they didn't want to be the next body lying dismembered on the bank of the Rio Grande as a warning to others. That was one way to leave the life of law enforcement. You had to choose: corruption, leaving entirely, or a shallow grave along the banks—a short-lived repose before the wild dogs dug you up and played with your bones.

The first thing Rico noticed was the smell. Corpses stink; he expected that. What he wasn't expecting was the terrible rotting seaweed stench mixed with the sickly vinegar smell of heroin. The black, sticky tar stuff. It wasn't new, and they had found shipments of the shit before. Usually, he would box it up, put it in evidence, and within a week, someone had made it "disappear"—back into the hands of the cartels, no doubt.

But this wasn't a shipment; it was a body. Waterlogged and slightly bloated, the corpse of a young Mexican man lay on the shore torn apart. Rico paused; he wouldn't say that the cartel hits weren't that vicious, but usually, you could see what they did. They used blades and guns, car batteries and acid. They didn't tear the bodies apart.

And this fucker was torn the fuck apart.

Beto started puking as soon as he saw the body. Rico felt queasy too but managed to hold down his lunch. It was surreal, like someone wanted to find out how bad you could abuse a corpse. He had seen only one corpse in this bad of shape, and that was when a drug dealer had fed a woman to his pet alligators.

Even still, this was worse. On top of the physical damage, there were weird things growing in his body; it looked like river grass and mold filling his lungs and stomach. Black sludge oozed from the corners of his mouth, the source of the spoiled wine smell.

And then the scavengers. Salamanders and axolotls were not rare, but it was far from common to see them outside the water. The body was swarming with them. The things were chewing the skin, crawling into the open wounds, and devouring the disgusting malformed innards. There were even small ones emerging from his nose to lap at the tar-like ooze that was still bubbling up from his mouth. Rico had always assumed the things were herbivores, or that they ate bugs, but they were going to town. Maybe they'd just never gotten a chance; usually, vultures would be swarming this body, but for some reason, there were none within sight. Rico scanned the horizon. Maybe there was a better meal somewhere else, or maybe the birds saw the diseased meat and refused to eat it. But for whatever reason, they were gone and nature had provided a different scavenger.

Manni went over to the body and starting kicking at the little lizards, trying to shoo them back into the water. The little fuckers hissed at him, swiped their glistening claws at him. At first, he laughed—the absurdity of these little bastards trying to defend their meal against a full-sized human seemed ludicrous. But Manni kept it up; he landed a solid kick into the side of one of the lizards, and it exploded! A puff of pink and red mist was all that was left once his steel-toed boot made contact with it. The other creatures finally reacted then—skittering backwards, hissing and snapping at Manni as they retreated.

He turned to the group of men and flexed, putting on a show for their laughter.

He shouldn't have.

While his back was turned to the body, another of those things, an axolotl, crawled out of the body cavity. It was huge compared to the smaller ones, almost the size of a cat. It launched at Manni, landing on his back. Rico and the others just kept laughing—if anything, they laughed harder. The thing looked ridiculous, frills and weird bug eyes; it didn't look dangerous. And Manni was screaming. Rico thought he was screaming because he was startled; it just made him laugh harder. But then Manni started convulsing and spinning, trying to rip the thing off his back, and the men stopped laughing when they saw the thing was actually digging through his shirt and tearing through his skin. A waterfall of blood drenched his back, and bone was visible through the ragged flaps of flesh that the creature had torn loose.

It was one thing to see a mutilated corpse; it was another thing entirely to see the mutilation happening. It was horrific. Rico was frozen, his mind emptied of action by the sheer terror he felt. Should he try to rip the thing off Manni's back? Should he shoot? Miguel ended up breaking free of the fear first. He ran up, grabbed the thing, and pulled it off Manni's back, along with a lot of Manni's skin. Gobs of flesh, shredded meat, fell to the ground along with the creature. Beto was still puking; Rico ignored the worthless asshole, drew his sidearm, and started shooting. He wasn't the best shot in the world, but he had been in the army for a few years before going into the federal police force and being stationed at the border so knew how to handle a gun. Rico put a few bullets in the thing, but the creature shrugged the bullet fire off and started scrabbling towards him. Rico's scream was high and shrill as he backpedaled away from the thing. Miguel pulled out his gun and started shooting too.

Somewhere in the back of Rico's mind, he realized the ridiculousness of the situation: four adult men, trained police, panicking—one of them bleeding out, one of them puking, and two of them shooting like maniacs at a lizard the size of a cat. It was humiliating, and Rico was secretly happy there was no one else there to see his panic.

Finally, the thing stopped coming at them; it just collapsed to the ground and started spasming as it died. When it stopped moving, Rico went over to it to kick at the remains, some part of him curious if it would explode into mist too but also just to show it who was boss. Manni started screaming again, this time at Rico.

"I need to go to the hospital! Take me to the hospital! I need help, help me!" The words tumbled out of him, starting high and loud and losing steam as he spoke. His face looked waxy and pale; his eyes were unfocused, rolling in his head. It was obvious the man was in shock. Miguel stepped forward and hooked his hands under Manni's armpits and started to pull him off the ground.

"Ah fuck!" Miguel said.

Rico turned to see the fucking things coming out of the water—more of those frilled lizards coming to eat the body and probably the one they had killed. Rico ran. He didn't wait to watch what the things did. He reached the truck first and jumped in the driver seat, then stuck his head out the window.

"Put them in the bed!" he shouted back.

"The back? Why?" Miguel asked, dragging Manni, manhandling him to the bed of the truck.

"Why? Because he's fucking bleeding everywhere and Beto won't stop throwing up."

Miguel nodded and hefted Manni into the truck as

gently as was possible. Rico was glad Miguel was part of the team; he was built like a Luchador and didn't ask a lot of stupid questions.

"I'm done throwing up," Beto argued.

"Fuck you, you're covered in vomit; get in the back," Rico growled. "And you can watch Manni and make sure he's okay."

Beto relented and climbed into the back of the truck. Rico didn't waste any time; as soon as Miguel hopped into the truck, he took off. The hospital was a pretty serious drive. Rico didn't feel any guilt for putting Beto in the back. He understood—they were all affected by the nightmarish gore and violence, turning their stomachs and making their bile rise—but Beto's stink and the gagging noises would have just sent them all over the edge.

2.

WHEN THEY GOT to the hospital, both Beto and Manni were looking worse for it. Beto was nearly green with how sick he was, leaning over the edge of the bed, barely able to keep his head up. But Manni must have lost a lot of blood because he was pale, almost white. His eyes were bloodshot, and he was drooling a thick string of pinkish phlegm. Rico thought maybe the axolotl cut into his lungs, but at least he was still alive—maybe he didn't want to be, but he was.

They got them both checked in with the usual method: waving a badge around, demanding special treatment. Sometimes Rico felt like shit doing that sort of thing. But at the same time, it was the police putting their asses on the line, and Rico believed they deserved some special treatment for painting targets on their backs for the cartel. Beto was walked back to get IV fluids, but they wheeled Manni back towards the emergency treatment rooms quick as can be. Rico watched them go and then sat heavily in one of the waiting room chairs next to Miguel.

Rico decided to call brass and explain what happened; after all, they had just left the body there, the whole reason they went to the river, and they didn't even take care of it. But what choice did they have? Shit had hit the fan, and all he could do was roll with the punches.

He got reamed out over it.

"What do you mean you didn't retrieve the body?" The voice on the other end of the phone was Chief Rodrigo

"We were attacked! The things tore up Officer Espado; he's in the ER now."

"The things. The sirens?"

"Yes, sir."

"You must be completely full of shit, Sanchez; salamanders aren't aggressive. And even if they were, they couldn't do any harm."

"This thing was different, sir. It was huge; it had claws. They were fucked up, like mutated or something. It took several shots to bring it down."

"So you killed one of them?" the chief asked.

"Yes, we killed the one that attacked Espado, sir."

"Did you bring the body of the thing at least?"

Rico paused; he hadn't thought to do that. But if it were poisonous or had some specific toxin, the doctors might need it. Rico squeezed his eyes shut, frustrated that he had been so stupid as to leave the thing behind.

"No," he finally answered.

"Fuck, you fucking incompetent pieces of shit. Let me talk to the doctor!"

Rico did as he was told, flagging down a nurse to fetch the doctor and finally handing the phone off. He stood there awkwardly, watching as the doctor walked away with his phone to have a whispered conversation with Chief Rodrigo. Finally, the doctor walked back, handed him the phone without a word, and walked off.

"Hello?" Rico asked, seeing if the chief was still on the line.

"Listen, Sanchez—Rico . . . " He sounded subdued, almost cowed. "I need you to listen to me. I need all of you to keep your mouths shut on this. Don't tell anyone what you saw or what happened; keep everything between you and the doctors. Do you understand?"

"Uh, yessir," Rico mumbled, looking over at Miguel. He knew he could trust Miguel, but could he trust the idiot Beto? And if Manni survived, he would be drugged up; would he even be able to keep from talking when they had him on morphine?

"Good, I'll have . . . someone come in for a debrief. Stay put."

The line went dead, and Rico's blood went cold.

Stay put. That was an ominous order. Rico's mind raced as he tried to think about what could be going on. Maybe it was some sort of endangered animal thing, or maybe something crazier. Rico thought about his son, who loved those sci-fi movies. Garbage, sure, but it made him think about stuff like government conspiracies. Maybe those things were genetically altered.

He sat back down next to Miguel.

"Fuck."

"They mad?" Miguel asked.

"Yes, they are mad," Rico responded, rubbing his eyes. He dropped down to a whisper. "Rodrigo said not to tell anyone what happened and that someone is coming to . . . debrief us."

Miguel's eyes darted to the door. Rico could see his mind working overtime and imagined that Miguel was thinking the same thing he was. They were in trouble.

Yeah, they were both federales, but they weren't untouchable. They could get got by common gangsters, civvies with a stick up their ass, or, more likely, by other federales above them in the pecking order. It wasn't a secure life they were leading. So they sat there whispering in the corner like school children afraid that the teacher would overhear them.

"Maybe it's one of ours," Miguel suddenly said, dropping his voice even lower.

"What?" Rico asked, leaning forward to hear him. "You mean a border police?"

"No, like someone that the government wanted gone."

It wasn't a pretty thing, but it *was* an undeniable truth; their government had its share of corruption. As much as Rico liked pointing a finger at the Americans and shouting about their fucked system, he knew that the cartels wouldn't have such power if it wasn't subsidized by government officials. That was another thing they had to deal with: how do you fight a war on a crime when your bosses were in the pockets of the enemy general?

Rico considered what Miguel was suggesting, and he didn't like it—not at all—but his mind kept rolling back to those shitty sci-fi movies, the ones with giant spiders and two-headed sharks. None of them had ever seen animals like that, and Miguel had lived his whole life on the banks of the river. Rico also remembered the way the killed man looked so fucked up, like he had things growing inside him, a disease eating away at what was human in him.

The two men fell quiet as they waited. Everything seemed surreal in that moment. Their quiet contemplation was shattered as Beto came back, looking much better than he had when he left.

"Beto," Rico said, the cold weight in his gut telling him the answer before he even asked the question. "Did you say anything? Tell anyone what we saw?"

Beto looked at Rico as if he had grown another head. "Of course I did! It was so fucked up, and I didn't want the nurses thinking I was some asshole who couldn't handle a corpse or something."

"Fuck, you *are* an asshole!" Miguel growled.

Rico nodded; nurses couldn't keep their traps shut. Within a few hours, everyone in this hospital would have heard the news, and it would spread from there. It would definitely get back to the brass.

"Chief Rodrigo specifically told us to keep our mouths shut, idiot," Rico whispered, taking some pleasure in the way Beto went pale, looking like he would vomit again. Rico didn't usually have to worry too much about getting killed by his own employers, but being a big mouth was a good way to cash in on permanent retirement early.

They fell into a silence that none of them wanted to break. Rico was considering his own mortality; he assumed the others were doing the same. He wondered if Manni was going to make it. When they were taking him out of the bed of the truck, he had been completely out of it, his head rolling around like a ragdoll.

They were still sitting around silently hours later when a man in a well-fitting suit and two men in full combat gear entered the doors of the hospital. Rico swallowed; this was it. The man scanned the waiting room, saw the three of them, and then walked to the receptionist. After a few minutes of speaking, he waved the two soldiers down the hall and turned towards them. Rico looked away quickly, trying to make it seem like he hadn't been staring, that he wasn't shitting myself.

The man approached them and stood there, arms crossed over his chest as if waiting for them to fess up that they had talked to the civvies and fucked everything up. None of them recognized the man; he wasn't from the border police office. No one at their office could afford a suit that nice.

"What happened?" he asked, not bothering to introduce himself.

Rico glanced at Beto and Miguel, hoping they would answer, wishing anyone would answer other than him. But they stayed silent.

"I said, what happened." The man's voice had grown an edge, a sharp thing ready to slide across their throats and dump them in the desert.

"Just like I said on the phone," Rico said with a bravado he didn't feel, trying to hide his fear behind dismissiveness, a machismo that was a natural defense mechanism.

'I wasn't on the phone with you, so pretend I don't know anything and tell me what happened." The man snarled.

"We got called out to the river this morning—" Rico began, prepared to recount everything that had happened, when he was cut off by the sound of gunfire and a terrifying inhuman scream.

3.

CHAOS EXPLODED IN the hospital, civilians screaming and running from the sound of gunfire and whatever had made that horrible noise. The three federales and the man in the suit didn't run, though God knew Rico wanted to. Miguel's gun was in his hand faster than Rico could believe. Beto was scrambling for his sidearm, and Rico's hand was resting on his. It gave him a second of relief; whatever was happening, he and Miguel were ready. Or so he thought.

One of the soldiers who had gone back exploded through the doors leading into the waiting room, running full tilt. He tripped over himself and sprawled onto the ground, his rifle spinning across the tiles. Rico didn't have time to wonder what he was running from as the answer presented itself almost immediately.

The thing that pushed through the door was a nightmare made manifest. It stood on two legs and wore a tattered hospital gown like a man, but its veins pulsed with a terrible pink light, giving its skin an infected, irritated look. Its legs ended in bird-like feet, each toe tipped with a cruel talon, and the arms that hung limply at its side were covered in bony growths that reminded Rico of a cricket's jagged, chitin-covered legs. The face was the worst part, though. Infected-looking flesh covered a too-wide head, like someone had taken a human skull and stretched it out horizontally in order to fit in a horrible toad mouth and then filled that mouth with a possum's needle-like teeth.

Its eyes were bright red and protruded from either side of the thing's skull. They blinked unevenly as it turned its head this way and that to look at the men. A third eye opened in the middle of its face, between the stretched nostrils, tearing the flesh open in a splash of glowing blood. This new eye regarded them with hunger and malice.

Its throat expanded like a toad's, and then it opened its horrendous mouth wide and emitted a rasping croak of a roar that caused the windows in the waiting room to rattle.

The soldier scrambled across the floor, reaching for his gun, but the creature wasn't going to give him a chance. It leapt forward, easily clearing the ten feet of space between them, and landed on the soldier's back and bit into the man, its wide mouth easily engulfing his entire shoulder. With a wrenching pull, the creature tore the man's arm off and gulped it down into its gullet, its terrible eyes pushing down into its skull to force the meat of its victim down its throat.

"FUCK FUCK FUCK!" Rico heard the screamed profanity before he even realized it was his voice. He bit down on his tongue, not wanting to draw attention from the monster. The images of those sci-fi movies flooded back into his mind. His gun was in his hand—he didn't remember drawing it, but he was already firing, each squeeze of the trigger accompanied by a shout,

Bang! "FUCK!"

Bang! "FUCK!"

Bright pink wounds were opening on the thing's flesh, splotches of luminescent blood spreading across the hospital gown, as the three men emptied their magazines into the monster. It wasn't enough. They hadn't reloaded since the incident on the banks of the river when they had torn the cat-sized axolotl apart with gunfire. It screamed at them.

Rico realized that the empty click of his weapon was no longer drowning out his expletives. He continued to pull the trigger anyway, his brain unwilling to accept that he was now defenseless in the face of this creature.

It screamed again at them, bits of flayed flesh and goblets of meat spraying from its mouth as it intoned its terrible cry over the body of the soldier that was convulsing in death throes. Rico stared at it, then saw the rifle the soldier had dropped. Maybe he could get to it while the monster tore the dying man apart. He took a step forward but then froze as the creature looked up at him, its head tilting as if it were considering what it wanted to do: eat the corpse at its feet or attack Rico.

Whatever intelligence worked behind those terrible red eyes seemed to connect the pain of its wounds with the four men, and it howled, taking a staggered step forward. Rico watched, unable to move no matter how hard his brain was screaming at his legs to carry him far away from this nightmare. The four men watched transfixed as the thing took another step forward and then fell forward, succumbing to its wounds.

Rico let out a shuddering sigh, relief filling him. "What the fuck is that?" He meant to shout it, to let out his fear in a bellow of outrage, but the words whispered out of him as a rasp.

"A big fucking problem, brother," Miguel said calmly. Rico was envious of Miguel's calm.

"That was . . . above your paygrade." The man in the suit turned to face them. "But we need to get out of here."

"Fuck you, man. Manni is still back there, and it's dead." Beto's voice shook like a virgin on his first trip to a brothel, and Rico was actually grateful for it. Beto's naked fear and plainly false bravado made Rico look better by comparison, but he did have a point.

"We can't leave him."

"He's dead," the man in the suit said. "Or worse."

"Worse?" Beto asked.

"How do you know he's dead?" Miguel asked at the same time.

"I don't have time for this shit. Either we can go now, or I can—"

Whatever he was about to say was cut off by another scream, inhuman and rasping, from beyond the now busted doors leading deeper into the hospital.

The man didn't answer, instead turning and running for the door. Rico and Miguel looked at each other before following suit. Whatever those things were, Rico didn't want to hang around and find out. But he did make a detour, grabbing the rifle off the ground—an FX-05 Xiuhcoatl assault rifle made there in Mexico for use by the military. Rico was relieved; he knew the gun from his time in the army. He considered checking the corpse to see if he had more ammo on him, but the sound of scrabbling and screeching from beyond the broken doors made him think better of it, and he followed Beto and Miguel out into the parking lot.

Rico ran up to the three men, wondering why they were just standing there, when he heard another inhuman cry. But instead of coming from inside the hospital, it was coming from in front of them. His eyes scanned the rows of parked cars, his heart thudding against his ribs so hard he felt like it might burst through his chest. There it was. This one was different.

The one inside had looked like a deformed pink frog. The thing in front of them, perched on the dented roof of their truck, look like someone had wrapped human skin around a monstrous grasshopper. Barbs stuck out of its forearms and legs. Its eyes, throbbing and pink, had grown to dominate the majority of the thing's face, and the most sickening detail had to be the blood-splattered bone mandibles that had torn out its face.

But worst of all, the thing was wearing clothes.

Rico didn't hesitate. He brought the barrel of the gun up and took aim. The kickback into his shoulder was incredible. So much power, so much killing force. He continued to spray bullets, shouting a wordless barbaric yawp as he did. Glass shattered, holes were punched into cars, but with so many bullets spitting out so quickly, many found their homes in the mutated flesh of the creature. It went down after the second bullet found its skull and blew out its eye, glowing pink blood and grey goop splattering the cars behind it. In the low evening light, it made the parking lot look like a poorly decorated discotheque.

Rico lowered the rifle and let out another shout. "Fuck yeah!" He turned to look at Miguel and Beto, his ecstasy of the kill flowing out of his body in a torrent as he saw both men firing at more creatures. They were emerging from the hospital now, crawling over cars, coming for them.

"Fuck, stop shooting! We need to go!" The man in the suit was shouting at them.

Rico didn't want to stop shooting—that was the last thing he wanted to do—but it made sense. The man was already running towards a sleek, black Range Rover. Rico glanced back at their truck—he had shot it up; it wouldn't be starting. He grabbed Beto's arm and dragged him towards the man's SUV. "Miguel! Let's go!"

Miguel glanced back at him and then at the oncoming horde emerging from the hospital. It looked like something out of an aliens movie. They skittered across the walls, malformed fingers with too many joints. And all of their terrible eyes, which pulsed with sickening light, were fixed on them. Miguel spat a curse and turned to join their flight to the car.

The man hardly waited for all three of them to get in before he hit the gas and catapulted them forward. Swerving around parked cars, he screeched out of the parking lot and spared no time in putting space between them and the hospital. Miguel, from the front seat, turned and lifted his gun to point at the man's temple.

"Who the fuck are you? What the fuck was that?" he growled.

The man glanced over at Miguel and frowned, then calmly turned his eyes back to the road.

"You didn't say please."

"Fuck you!" Miguel screamed, his nerves getting the better of him. "Answer the fucking question, asshole!"

"My name is Chief Inspector Alejandro Cazalla. I'm with the PFM." He glanced at Miguel and his gun again. "And what that was is a national crisis."

"National?" Beto stuttered from the back seat, where he was curled into a nearly fetal ball.

"Yes, these things. People are turning into these things in hospitals all over the country," Alejandro said with a grim smile. "And we have no idea why."

4.

JUST OUTSIDE THE RUINS OF AUSTIN, TEXAS

THE ABHORRENT WAS unaware of the name that the humans had given it. It was barely aware of their presence. Their super structures and buildings barred its path. Their dams created pools for it to refresh in. Of course, in San Antonio, one of the first major hubs of humanity it had crossed, the humans had fought back. At first, it had been confusing for the massive axolotl; the bullets meant nothing to it, too small to penetrate its slick slime-covered flesh. The missiles and rockets, on the other hand, had been an irritant.

Would San Antonio have been completely crushed under the creature's heels had the humans not antagonized the Abhorrent? It was impossible to know, for the Abhorrent was not cognizant of the damage it caused, only that it had been hurt and would respond as violently as it needed to in order to end any threat. But even if the Abhorrent hadn't thrashed around and lashed out in a show of goliath destruction, the masses of afflicted humans and animals that swarmed around its feet would have brought the city to its knees.

As was evident when, only a few days later, the terrible parade of mutated monsters reached Austin under the frilled banner of the Abhorrent. The military was still scrambling to figure out how to stop the monster and its army, but they knew without a shadow of a doubt that the thing wasn't deterred by tanks or missiles. Perhaps evacuation would have saved lives, but the city was already in chaos from the afflicted that ran rampant across the streets and through the homes and high-rises of the city.

The behemoth trudged through the southern reaches of the city, having followed the path of Edward's Aquifer from the San Antonio River using senses that were impossible to define in human terms. It slipped into Lady Bird Lake, too shallow, too small to contain its full bulk, and the pinkish miasma that dripped from between its lipless maw floated across the water like an infected fog. The creatures in its wake—a plethora of things that had once been part of the natural Texas ecology but were now metamorphosed into a nightmare horde serving as the vanguard of the Abhorrent—swarmed across the I35 bridge and the lake, a tidal wave of tortured flesh storming into the city proper.

The Abhorrent watched from its aquatic perch as the city of Austin burned, screams and sirens echoing over the skyline. The people had weathered the first storm of afflicted with *only* several hundred thousand dead, having fled, armed to the teeth, to the relative safety of towering buildings that looked like half-mast erections puncturing the sky. But now an army was at the gates. The afflicted where no longer just mutated humans but coyotes, deer, cows, and monstrous birds that all flocked to the warmth of the meat of the living humans.

And those who were able to fight off the afflicted lost not their lives but their humanity as the Abhorrent rose from Lady Bird Lake and began its slow, ponderous walk through the city. The monstrosity had no knowledge of the death and destruction that wallowed in its footsteps, only that something was pulling it ever farther north and the structures that stood in its way fell too easily to its claws.

PART 2:

WAR

UMANITY FELL INTO familiar tropes. Post-apocalyptic and zombie movies had taught us what to do. We fortified areas of town we thought were safe. We delved head-first into xenophobia, but without the media to fear monger, most of our anger was directed at the afflicted and not each other. For the most part.

We still had conspiracy theorists and right-wing provocateurs, but without national television screaming at us every night that we were our own enemies, we were able to focus on the things outside the gates that were trying to kill us. Those whose focus was turning us against ourselves and seizing some sort of power were still present, but they were confined to the outposts and fortified areas they had found. Their influence was limited, in most cases.

Of course, in some of the bigger cities, or cities with a military presence, things were very different. While Texas and Northern California (not to mention much of the area between the two states) were devastated by the mutated kaiju that eventually tore into each other, most cities only had to deal with the human and animal-sized afflicted—things that could be fought, things that could be killed.

The military protected themselves first and foremost, and while I can't say that I blame them, forgiveness comes hard for many. People want to know why it took so long for the armed forces to save them, why so many people died. And most of all, they want the surviving generals and decision-makers to stand trial and pay for what they did in the name of containment. Maybe they should; maybe they will.

But it will not change the cost in lives that was paid during those days.

Alexander Fienkolt
University of Texas, Archivist

SHIFTING ALLIANCES
FREDERICO SANCHEZ

5.

RICO WATCHED AS Inspector Cazalla flew down the highway towards Chihuahua, the nearest city.

"I was dispatched from Aerea Militar number 13," he explained. "We have seen these creatures, the mutations in the city, but have been able to contain them. This, however, was worse. Whatever is happening, it has something to do with the hospitals. We'll go ahead report to my captain, and once you are debriefed, we will decide what to do."

"What do you mean, what to do, asshole?" Miguel asked from the back seat.

"I mean that this is classified information. If word was to spread, there would be panic. It would be very bad for everyone involved, understand?" He shifted gears, picking up the pace, agitated by Miguel's animosity, as they entered the city. "So you may need to wait until we understand how to—"

"Hey, Inspector, that may not be a concern anymore," Rico said, staring out the passenger side window.

All the men fell silent as they saw more of the creatures, the mutated things, outside. In the hospital, it had been a horror show as the creature had eaten the soldier, and then again as they surrounded them in the parking lot. But now they were seeing a massacre as the things tore into civilians.

"Fuck," Beto whispered, his eyes wide. "I thought you said this was only happening at hospitals."

"I didn't say that," Cazalla muttered. He didn't sound as cocky and sure of himself as he had only a few seconds ago.

"The fuck you didn't," Rico growled. "You said this was happening at hotels across the country." He tried to control the hysteria that was creeping into his voice, but his throat was tight, and he could feel the ice-cold fingers of panic closing in around his heart, making his chest ache with every heartbeat.

"I said it was happening at the hospitals. Does it look like we contained it? Does it look like these fucking things just stay put? We're trying—"

"Look out!" Miguel shouted, dragging everyone's attention back to the road.

One of the creatures had moved into the street, dragging the body of an old woman by her leg. The thing that had once been a man was bent nearly in half, his legs bent backwards. Terrible claws emerged from his hands, twitching as he watched the oncoming car. His mouth stretched open, revealing rows and rows of jagged round teeth.

Cazalla hit the brakes, causing the car to skid to a halt; the smell of burning rubber filled their nostrils. The man thing tilted its head, watery eyes that seemed to sit poorly in his skull trying to make sense of the car. It dropped the corpse of the woman and leapt forward, landing on the hood of the vehicle, intent on taking on this new challenger.

"Drive! Drive! Drive!" Beto screamed.

Rico lifted his gun, but Cazalla grabbed his arm as he hit the gas, launching them forward.

"Idiot! You shoot from in here and it can get in!" the man growled as he swerved wildly, trying to throw the monster off the hood.

The car flew down the street and fishtailed around a turn. Rico's eyes were stuck on the monster in front of him. He considered rolling down the window and shooting that way, but the idea of exposing himself to the elements was terrifying. The creature's nails dug into the hood, shredding the metal as it tried to retain its purchase. Finally, Cazalla hit the brakes. The car skidded to a halt, but the creature lost its grip as its inertia carried it off the hood and sent it spinning into the street.

Cazalla gunned the car again, making them lurch forward, He aimed the car and smashed into the thing as it was pulling itself off the asphalt. There was sickening crunch as it was crushed beneath them.

"Hell yeah!" Cazalla laughed, looking out the back window at the twitching corpse of the monster. His laughter died in his throat as he caught sight of Rico pointing his pistol directly at his head.

"We're getting my family."

"What? The fuck we are; we need to get to the base." Cazalla scowled and looked back towards the street. He was trying to play it cool, but Rico could see the sweat beading on his forehead.

"Listen to me, motherfucker. Those things aren't at the hospital; they are on the street. And we aren't going anywhere without my fucking family. Now you can drive there, or I can blow your fucking brains out and drive there myself. Those are the choices, but we are going to go get my wife and my kids."

"Think, man, if those things are there, they are already—"

"Say that my family is dead," Rico whispered, pressing the barrel of his gun into Cazalla's temple. "Say it. See what happens next."

"Rico," Beto said from the back seat.

"Shut up, Beto; we're checking on Rico's kids." Miguel cut him off.

Cazalla glanced in the review mirror at the other two men and shook his head. "It's on your head," he muttered. "How do we get there?"

ABHORRENT ACCORDS

Getting to Rico's house was more difficult than he had anticipated, and not only because of the monsters that seemed to be swarming all over Chihuahua. Cazalla was just hitting them now, swerving to avoid those that ran at them and running over those that wouldn't get out of the way. Rico was grateful for the big SUV's mass. It plowed over the afflicted monsters with no problem. No, the difficulty was the other cars on the road, both abandoned and occupied. The entire time, Rico prayed that they wouldn't be too late, that they weren't rushing and endangering their lives for no reason. He prayed that when they got to Rico's apartment, there would be no monsters in sight. He stopped praying when they reached the apartment. There was no reason to keep going.

God wasn't listening to his prayers. Either God didn't exist or he was being flooded by the joint prayers of every person living through this nightmare. Which one it was didn't matter to Rico right then; all that mattered was reaching his family, a task that seemed impossible now. The apartment complex was anything but silent. Mutated creatures crawled over the walls, and Rico saw one pushing through a third story window. There were at least five of the things visible; he couldn't begin to guess how many more were inside. The monsters weren't looking at the car; they looked like they were bickering with each other, fighting over territory or food.

Rico bolted out of the car to the shouts and screams of his companions. Miguel reached out to try to stop him, but Rico's desperation made him faster. Rico didn't care how likely it was that he would die before he reached his front door; he only cared about getting inside to his son, to his daughters. He didn't look left or right as he darted across the lawn and slammed into the front doors of the building with his shoulder. He could hear the hissing of monsters, the discordant screams of the creatures suddenly becoming aware of new prey.

Rico slammed the doors closed behind him and rushed through the hallway, gun up and swinging wildly, terrified that each doorway would hold the creature that would leap out and take him out of the equation before he could get to his family. If he could just get to them, he could protect them, he could get them to the military where they would be safe. Up the three flights of stairs he flew, terrified the entire way that the next corner would reveal some terrifying monster. He heard them behind the doors he passed. They screeched and roared from people's private apartments, but were they the newly turned, or were they invaders that had come in and devoured the families within? Rico didn't dare answer that question.

Finally, he reached his door. He skidded to a halt and pushed his ear against the door to listen. He didn't hear screaming. He didn't hear either of his infant daughters crying either. He was relieved; if his daughters were asleep, their cries wouldn't attract any of the monsters. He unlocked the door and pushed it open.

The silence was no longer relieving. A cold dread gripped his heart, strangling his breath in his lungs as he looked over the scene of grisly carnage that painted the small kitchen and hallway. His wife's torso lay across their small dining table. Her mouth gaped open, and her dead eyes stared at him as if blaming him for not being here, not saving her. He didn't know where her arms were, but he could see a bloody onesie poking out from under the table. He could hear the ragged breathing of something.

No part of him wanted to look under the table; his daughter's clothes lay there, promising him that only death and despair lay in looking. But his wife . . . his wife's gaze held him; it demanded that if he couldn't save them, he could at least avenge them. Rico gritted his teeth and slowly squatted down, leveling his gun under the table; but when he was able to see more, all he could do was wail. A monster wearing his son's favorite transformers shirt crouched there in the middle of a puddle of gore and intestines, chewing on the face of an infant. The creature was more human than many of the monsters they had seen. Its head was hairless and sported bony ridges and spines. It eyes drooped in loose sockets as the creature's face seemed to sag under the weight of its own skin.

Hearing Rico's wail, the creature, his son, looked up, pulling the meat of the child's cheek with it until the skin snapped.

"Paaaaah aaaah," the creature whispered, locking eyes with Rico. "PAAH!" it roared as spat out its sister's face and charged forward towards its father.

Rico scrambled back with the horrifying realization that this wasn't some inhuman monster; this was his son, his boy, his pride that was scrambling towards him on gangly talon-tipped fingers and toes.

The gunshot retort tore through the air. Before Rico could understand what had happened, a bullet wound blossomed on his son's chest, the force of the bullet throwing him back, where he quivered and spasmed.

"No! Gabriel!" Rico crawled forward toward where he had fallen, but someone grabbed him around the neck and pulled him back.

Miguel had him in a headlock, restraining him. "Brother, we have to go!" He wrenched Rico around and pushed him towards the door, where he saw the inspector standing with a still-smoking gun.

"That was my son, you son of a bitch!" Rico launched himself towards the man, but Miguel grabbed him again.

"Rico, stop!"

"That wasn't your son! Not anymore!" Cazalla said. "I'm sorry."

"That was my boy. My son. My family." Rico collapsed into Miguel's arms.

"Not anymore. We have to go." Coldly, cruelly, Cazalla holstered his gun and turned to run back towards the car.

"Fucker," whispered Miguel. "He wanted to leave you. Beto's watching the car, keeping a gun on Cazalla so he can't leave us. Come on, brother. You can't help them now." He pulled Rico up and slipped his arm under Rico's armpits to support him and guided him back down to the car.

6.

THE CAR RIDE towards the army base was anything but calm and peaceful. The monsters were everywhere in the city, and the people of Chihuahua were reacting in a panic. There were also the opportunists—or would-be opportunists, anyway—people who thought that the chaos of the attack would grant them the opportunity to loot. Maybe some even succeeded, but they saw too many broken and partially devoured corpses hanging from windows and on the sidewalks next to shattered TVs, game consoles, and appliances. Everywhere they looked, there was chaos and pain, terror and bloodshed. As much as it pained Miguel, they couldn't get out and help anyone without forfeiting their own lives and safety.

But for Rico, the drive was a blur. He couldn't focus on what was happening. When he closed his eyes, all he could see was the mutated, sagging face of his son tearing into the angelic face of his daughter. And his wife's eyes. Even lifeless, they spoke an ocean of grief and rage into his soul, condemning him as a terrible husband, father, and man. And when his eyes were open . . . then all he could do was look next to him, at Cazalla, at the man who had murdered his son.

Part of him thought he was being unfair; that wasn't his son, it was a monster that had killed his boy, his girls, his woman. But that part was swallowed in grief, in denial. What was this terrible disease that was changing people into monsters? Why was it spreading? But mostly, was there a cure? A cure that would have brought his son back to him if Cazalla hadn't killed him? There was no way to know. Everything was twisted and terrible. He was vaguely aware that around them, the world was falling apart, that the city was more overrun, that it was swarming with monsters. In the matter of a few short hours, the outbreak had gone from isolated incidents at hospitals to something far more apocalyptic.

"It has to be an invasion, right?" Beto was saying as they peeled down an empty stretch of street. At that point, the sight and avoidance of the monsters was almost background noise. The vastness of what was happening taking their fear and pushing it towards dumbfounded shock. It was all they could do to try to rationalize what was happening, to make some sort of sense out of the senseless. "Aliens, you know, they probably hid at hospitals disguised as doctors and did experiments to make us into monsters; now it's on!"

"What aliens, idiot? These are people. Fuck, it's probably like Spider-Man," Miguel said.

"The fuck are you talking about?" Cazalla asked, glancing back at him in the rearview mirror.

"Those fucking lizards at the river, man, remember? They had glowing blood just like that fucker we shot at the hospital, just like all of these fucking monsters."

"The hell does that have to do with fucking Spider-Man?" Beto asked, completely lost.

"Man, you're stupid," Miguel spat. "Think about it. The spider bit Spider-Man and made him mutate into a superhero. Remember Manni was starting to look weird while we were taking them to the hospital. Maybe it's some, like, radioactive fucking lizard monsters."

"You think these things are superheroes?" Beto asked incredulously.

"No, fucker, it's an example. Like those things are causing people to change; more realistic than aliens," Miguel said. "What do you think, Rico?"

ABHORRENT ACCORDS

Rico didn't answer. He hadn't spoken since they left the apartment, he opened his eyes and stared down at his hands. He wasn't keeping up with their conversation; it was the buzzing of flies in his ears. He didn't look up when the car swerved or when Miguel rolled down the window to shoot at a monster that was clinging to the door. All of it was white noise that butted against the wall of grief that surrounded him. This wasn't the first time Miguel had tried to pull Rico into a conversation, but try as he might, he couldn't drag Rico out of his own cloud of misery.

Miguel let the question hang in the air, unable to pull it back. It sat there in the car like a fifth passenger, a critical mass of tension that increased the discomfort for everyone exponentially.

"They look like spiders more than lizards," Beto finally said, breaking the dense silence. "Maybe it's a government experiment gone wrong."

"Motherfucker!!" Cazalla spat. "We are the government! You think we would do this?"

"Man, we're the government the same way an ant is a colony. We ain't shit, not to them, hell." Miguel shot a hard look up at the driver. "We aren't shit to you; you were all set to leave—"

"Enough!" Cazalla interrupted, his hands gripping the steering wheel hard enough to make his knuckles go white. "No matter how you feel about our government, they wouldn't do this; we wouldn't do this!"

He made a hard right, turning onto the freeway that would lead right to the base. Outside of the city, there were fewer cars littering the road. The constant press of terrified people and monsters was left behind with the dense urban center.

Silence fell in the car again, each of the men thinking about the nature of the government. Would they create something like this? Mexico wasn't at war with anyone, other than the cartels; there was no need to develop such terrifying bioweapons as these. But what about the states?

Hadn't their president called Mexicans rapists and drug dealers? Hadn't they proposed a huge wall to separate the countries and then threatened to make Mexico pay for it? What if this was an attack not from some alien force but from their northern neighbors?

Only Rico was free of such rumination. His thoughts swam in a fog of outraged grief and powerlessness. He turned his eyes to the window, gazing out at the burning city. He remembered moving here, how his wife and he had argued so savagely about moving from their small village to the much bigger city. In the end, he had put his foot down; there was just nowhere to work, no opportunity to grow and succeed. And so they moved away from their families, away from what they knew. And what opportunities presented themselves in the city? They lived (had lived) in a too-small apartment; the kids attended (had attended) public schools. The only opportunity he had given his family was to be here, at ground zero, when the monsters came.

Cazalla had pulled the trigger, but Rico was responsible for his family being here in harm's way to begin with. He wanted to sink into the seat, to disappear and fade away into nothing. He wished Cazalla had left without him, that his son, Gilberto, had reached him, killed him, so he could have just died and been with his wife and children in heaven. Or maybe he *was* dead, dead and in hell.

"Demons," Rico whispered.

"What was that, brother?" Miguel asked.

"Demons," Rico said louder. "We're in hell, or hell is on Earth. It's obvious."

"It's obvious that these are demons from hell?" Cazalla scoffed, then fell silent at the terrible glare Rico gave him.

"Yeah, if you're not an imbecile. They possess humans, they become physical demons, they eat flesh, their blood glows. Even those lizards at the river, they were unnatural, monsters from hell. Mother of God, it is the end days and we are seeing the world covered in blood and fire." Rico's eyes glazed over as he spouted out the hodgepodge of spirituality and mysticism that he half-remembered from Sunday school and at his abuela's knee. "Santa Muerte laughs, and the possessed enact terrible violence on the innocent, spreading pain and suffering throughout the world. We are—"

"Shut the fuck up, Rico," Beto whispered hoarsely, his eyes wide with religious fear. "I'm not wicked; I'm not some criminal."

"No? When was the last time you went to confession, Beto? When was the last time you said your Hail Marys or gave tithe? I know it's been a goddamned long time for me." Rico's eyes lowered to his hands once more. It was a terrible thought, the ends times. There was no salvation coming for him, only hell on Earth and the demon sitting next to him that had killed his son.

"Oh fuck!" the demon snapped, forcing Rico's eyes back up.

There, ahead of them, was a long line of cars. Hundreds of vehicles all parked on the freeway, waiting for entry into the military base. It was no surprise; where else would people flock to when hell was unleashed? Who better to protect them when shit hit the fan than the people with guns and training? But these people would get no protection. Thick clouds of smoke filled the sky ahead of them, just above the roaring flames that were visible even with the miles separating them from the army base. He could see people climbing out of their cars, trying to march towards the inferno that was the army base, too stupid or too fearful to realize that the base was lost, that there would be no shelter or sanctuary within its burning walls.

7.

"**F**UCK," **MIGUEL SAID** under his breath a second before Cazalla unleashed a torrent of expletives that would make even Miguel pause. Rico just stared. Of course . . . of course the army of Mexico was already out of commission. What else could possibly happen when hell walked the earth on chitinous legs and drank in the ruined flesh of its people?

"What the fuck are we going to do now?" Miguel asked, watching the people marching to their doom. He was met with the desperate silence of men who had already given up and were resigned to sit in their car until the demons came to devour them.

"I have an idea," Beto finally said.

"Motherfucker, you do not!" Miguel fired back, the break in the settling tension enough to make him laugh.

"No, I do. I don't know if it's a good idea, but . . . "

"Just spit it out, asshole. Anything is better than sitting here and waiting for death," Cazalla said, though Rico didn't know if he agreed with the sentiment.

"We could go to La Tierra Abundante." Beto almost whispered it, knowing the reaction of his companions would be less than pleasant.

"Are you fucking crazy? Holy shit, Beto, there are bad ideas and then there is suicide! You want four cops to go knocking on Don Hernandez's door? And fucking say what?"

"And say we are there with a truce!" Beto cried. "Look,

who besides the military and the police have guns? The estate is far enough from the city limits that it won't be overrun."

Cazalla shook his head. "What kind of morons are they hiring for our police now?"

"You have a better idea?" Beto snapped, tired of being dismissed.

No one answered him.

They might have descended back into their sullen silence, but the now all-too-familiar sound of a discordant scream rent the air, pulling all of their attention to the road ahead of them.

More demons.

Were they coming from the base or emerging from the cars? Rico thought it must be the latter, as he could see a malformed bone-tipped limb punch through the roof of one of the cars in front of him. The inner windows were already coated with blood and gore, the remains of whatever family had been in the car with the demon. Farther ahead, he could see more of the creatures moving through the smoke, attacking cars and the people who had foolishly left the relative safety of their vehicles. How? How did the creatures spread so rapidly? Rico knew the answer: They were demons; demons were not constrained by the rules of humanity, physics, nature. The only rule they followed was that of bloodshed.

The creature in the car ahead of them punched another bone-talon through the roof of the car and began ripping the steel apart. The four men watched, almost entranced, as the creature tore its way free from the car and stretched out. Beto let out a whimper. They knew it had once been human, but if they hadn't seen the metamorphosis themselves, it would have been impossible to guess. Blood-crusted skin stretched over unnaturally elongated limbs. The fingers and toes had fused, creating spikes of bone and keratin. Its face looked like the skull had stretched, elongating into something more equine, the sagging skin barely covering the low hanging jaw. Its maw couldn't close due to a plethora of needle-sharp teeth jutting at unnatural angles from the bleeding gums of the monster. The thing finished extracting itself from the roof of the car, the remains of what had been friends or family dripping from its mottled hide, and turned its malformed head to gaze at the four men.

"Fuck!" Cazalla threw the car into reverse and hit the gas, slamming them into the car that had come up behind. The men jerked with the impact, but there was no time to think. Cazalla quickly turned the wheel as far as it would go, shifted into drive, and stomped back on the gas, causing the vehicle to lurch forward and off the road. If any of the men could have stopped screaming as they watched the horse-demon clamber off the car and lope at a half gallop towards them, they might have been thankful they were in an all-terrain truck that could handle the rocky ground they now drove over.

Beto rolled down his window and fired back at the thing, but only two shots rang out before his firearm clicked empty. Too many casings littered the streets of Chihuahua, too many bullets fired with wild, fearful abandon that never found their mark.

Even with Beto's piss-poor aim, they increased the distance between them and this newest horror. Cazalla looked down at the gas gauge; it looked bleak. "We can't keep going forever. We'll run out of gas . . . "

"So stop for gas," Miguel grunted, his eyes still on the slowly shrinking figure of the monster that had been after them.

"So simple? Where? You think that tree over there offers petrol?" Cazalla said mockingly.

"Fuck you, man," Miguel spat. "There'll be stations once we get near a road again; don't be an asshole."

"And those stations may be empty, or broken, or have fucking monsters. No, we have enough to reach La Tierra Abundante. But that's it. You understand; you all understand. We get there, and if its fucked or if they turn us out, it's over. For all of us. You get that?"

"I don't know who you think you are, demon," Rico said softly, "but I haven't heard you offer a better plan. So maybe get off Miguel's nutsack and focus on driving."

Cazalla thought about offering some retort. He was used to being in charge, being in control, and, most of all, being feared. His gut reaction to Rico's insolent remark was to shout him down and threaten him. But the truth was that all of them sat in their own piss from fear-emptied bladders. He didn't feel strong or in control. He could bluster all he wanted, but in the end, he was just seeking some safe haven where he could crawl into a dark, lonely space and cry out his fear. So instead of getting into a shouting match with Rico, Cazalla stayed silent and did as he was told.

They drove for several miles across the stretch of wilderness, a drive made difficult as they picked their way through the terrain. But it was calmer now; they didn't see any of the monsters this far out of the city, which gave them even more hope that when they did get to their destination, it would indeed be a safe haven. After an hour of picking their way through the brush and country, Cazalla got them onto a dirt road and was able to make decent time towards the Hernandez estate, one eye on the dangerously low gas gauge the entire time.

No one commented about how well he seemed to know his way to the cartel leader's home.

There were no other cars on the road; no one was thinking to flee to the palace of a dangerous crime lord. Cazalla slowed down as he approached the front gates of the estate. They could all see the guards posted there and the fully automatic rifles the guards held pointed directly at them. One of the guards held out his hand, palm facing them, ordering them to stop. Cazalla slowly came to a halt and shut off the car before rolling down the window.

"Inspector," the guard greeted Cazalla, not lowering his weapon. "Hello."

"Hello," Cazalla responded, raising his hands to show they were empty.

"What are you doing here, Inspector? I think maybe the city needs you."

"The city is lost, my friend, the army base too . . . We knew that Don Hernandez would keep his home safe, that it would be safe. You know, we're all . . . all of us are trained soldiers. We can all fight, work; we can earn our keep." Cazalla was rambling.

The guard stepped back and radioed something. He stood there, his gun trained on Cazalla while the other guards kept their aims on the other three men. Finally, he must have gotten word back, as he approached the door once more.

"Any of you get bit?" he asked.

"Bit? What?" Cazalla asked.

"Yeah, bitten; how do you think this shit is spreading? You never watch a zombie movie, shit-fucker? Where any of you bitten?" The guard sounded on edge.

"No, man, none of us—"

"Cazalla was bitten," Rico suddenly said, cutting him off. "Back in the city. He was bitten."

"What the fuck, no—" Cazalla started to say, but he never finished as the guard fired three shots into the car, obliterating Cazalla's head. Shards of bone, teeth, and bits of brain showered the three men.

Rico stared straight ahead. He wanted to laugh; he wanted to cry. But he stayed silent.

"Anyone else?"

Slowly, Miguel leaned forward and whispered, "No, sir."

"Good. Get out of the car and come in. Keep your guns in the car and your hands where I can see them."

ABHORRENT ACCORDS

They had been frisked, questioned, and then, finally, led to separate rooms, where they were allowed to shower and clean up. Rico was sitting on the edge of the single bed, his eyes red, wondering why he still couldn't cry despite the massive weight of his grief, which felt like it would explode out of his chest, when there was a knock on the door.

"Enter."

The door opened, and another guard came in, his handgun trained on Rico. Behind him, an old man in a silk shirt and khaki pants and using a wooden cane followed. He was slightly overweight and looked to be in his early 60s. He didn't say anything at first, walking around the little room and looking it over, then he finally pulled a small wooden chair from the corner of the room and sat in front of Rico.

"We looked over Inspector Cazalla," Don Hernandez said without preamble.

Rico met his eyes but didn't respond. What could he say? He knew where this conversation was going.

"You know, to see for ourselves. But when we did our autopsy, we found no bites, not even any scratches. No, the only wounds were the ones that ended his life. Incredible, no?"

Rico looked down at his hands. Was this how he died? Sitting alone in a small room, executed for having another cop killed? Was Cazalla corrupt? It appeared so. Did he deserve to die? Absolutely. Rico finally looked up and met Hernandez's eyes.

"He shot my son; he killed my son." He choked on the words, trying to get them out from around the ball of hurt in his chest.

"Yes, your son was changed?" Hernandez asked.

Rico nodded.

"So he did the right thing."

Rico stiffened, but before he could respond, Hernandez held up a hand. "But even still, as a father . . . " He tapped his chest. "As a father, we can't live with that, eh? We can't allow that to go unanswered, even when it is the right thing. I understand." He rose and placed a hand on Rico's shoulder. "But now, no lies; there can be only truth between us, understand? This is the only way we survive; this is the only way we live here and make it to the end of the world."

Rico slowly nodded.

"Good. Come down in about an hour. We will have dinner, some coffee, and you and your friends can tell me what the hell is happening in the city." Don Hernandez stood and stretched, muttering something about his knees, then walked out of the room, his cane clicking with each step.

The guard followed after, never taking his eyes off Rico.

When they were gone, Rico was finally able to cry.

NORTHERN CALIFORNIA, THE REDWOOD FOREST

IT WAS NO longer safe in the forests of trees. They were too small; it could feel that they would no longer support its weight. So the creature—nearly four hundred tons of muscle, fur, and fury—crawled down to the forest floor and began moving to find a new place to nest. It's hands, tipped with massive curved claws, dug furrows in the dirt and asphalt with equal ease. And as it moved, a dark pink miasma leaked from between its needle-sharp, meter-long teeth. Its nose twitched; it could smell the stink of humanity and, more importantly, humanity's refuse.

There were people in the forest, people who thought they could escape the chaos of the cities, avoid the horrifying death that screamed at the door for meat and blood. They had been horrified to discover that the sickness, the affliction, wasn't confined to the cities, and not to humans either. An entire encampment of survivors from the city had been eviscerated and now played host to families of spider-like squirrels with clicking mandibles and a ravening hunger. But as the massive possum clawed its way free of the forest, pushing over towering Redwood trees and swatting parked vehicles out of its way, the squirrel-things knew that the best course of action was to follow. Thus the parade of the monstrous began its inexorable march southeast.

Behind the creature, its massive, hairless tail whipped through the air. Spines that had sprouted caught in trees, uprooting them as it passed, and with each passing moment, more mutated creatures joined its menagerie. It didn't mind the little things that ran under its feet; they were insignificant. It left the safety of the woods in the darkness of night, heading into a desert it would never have attempted to enter before its evolution. Hundreds of miles away, though, on the horizon, was a false dawn. The constant sound and glitz of human civilization. The city of humans was burning, and even from miles away, the creature's sensitive nose could smell the glorious aroma of open flesh.

In another life, the creature would have shunned human contact, sneaking into trashcans and dumpsters for a snack here and there. Now, something else clicked in its brain; a primordial aggression towards the tiny creatures filled its senses, and it became hunger incarnate.

Its hiss spread the pink mist far and wide as it charged into Las Vegas. The lights and colors were accented by the flames and screams, made ethereal by the thick smoke that rose from the burning city. Of course, Las Vegas was strewn with the entrails flung high into the sky by celebrant afflicted, those voracious mutants who had evolved with poison coursing through their veins. This only added to the creature's hunger. It was not an idle defender like the Abhorrent, who led its army passively, stomping the world into oblivion while oblivious to the damage it caused.

No, this new kaiju that emerged from the Redwoods of Northern California was driven to violence. It struck at the tall buildings and used its hands to grab swathes of living creatures from the ground and shoving them into its maw, picking afflicted and human alike from the debris like ticks from the fur to skewer on its sword like teeth. Something in its brain riled at the existence of the buildings, as though the very existence of humanity was an insult or possibly a threat.

Two days later, the possum, the nameless hunger embodied in the swollen flesh of a fledgling god, sat amongst the ruins of Las Vegas and considered. It was still hungry, still filled with rage and animosity. It caught a fleshy creature, swollen with malformed limbs, off the shattered pavement outside of the ruins of a false Roman palace and popped it like a grape between its jaws, slurping this viscous ichor that oozed from its snack as it considered its next actions. It had no plans, though part of it knew that shelter, food, and a mate were of utmost importance.

But something else called to it, a primal urge that tugged at some territorial instinct. It did not know why, but it lifted its terrible bulk and began to waddle through the desert, heading vaguely east, towards something it could not know was its destiny.

HIVE

8.

GILBERTO MEWED IN agony where he lay on the dirty tile of the Sanchez apartment's little kitchenette. His hand rose and prodded at the wound in his chest, all seven digits twitching as it took in the ragged flesh and the sticky oozing blood that coated him. The pain was unimaginable, but he remembered there were pain killers in the bathroom. Pills that Papa was prescribed recently for an old wound. Pills that Papa refused to take but that Gilberto had found and would take when his parents went to sleep. They killed the pain and made him feel funny but good funny, like the world was swimming around him. Those would stop the hurting. Gilberto turned himself over, screeching in pain as he did.

He could barely see through the folds of his face as the flesh covered his eyes, but he knew the way. He crawled, pulling himself by his splayed hands, the keratin claws clacking against the tile with each desperate grab. He could smell the sweet flesh of Mama and his sisters but would not be distracted. The pain was worse than the hunger. So he ignored the food for now as he made his way to the bathroom. Once there, he reached up and grasped the edge of the sink before pulling himself up.

It hurt so bad, and Gil was so scared, terrified really. He wailed for his mommy, forgetting for a moment that he had torn her intestines out to get to that delicious liver. Weeping thick, phlegmy tears, he mounted the sink, hunching over to keep his balance, and scrabbled at the latch of the cabinet with his claws. It took a few tries to get the door to swing open; his hands were designed for tearing and ripping, the extra fingers getting in his way as he tried fine manipulation. Was that like teeth? he wondered. Would he lose his baby fingers as his adult fingers came in?

The question melted from his brain as the cabinet swung open. He peered up, more to cause the loose skin around his eyes to rest in a way that didn't obscure his vision. So many delicious bottles, so many strange feelings. But now he just wanted the one that would make the ouchies go away. He pushed toiletries out of the way, ignoring the toothpaste and facial creams that his mother had spent her adulthood using to stave off the inevitable creep of aging. There, just where Gil had hidden it, was the small orange prescription bottle of hydrocodone.

He grabbed the bottle and, still perched on the edge of the sink, tore off the lid and poured the large oblong pills down his throat. He could feel the cilia in his throat pulling the pills down and into his stomach. He sat there like a gargoyle, perched on the stained porcelain pillar, his mind racing—anything to keep it off the owie in his chest. He was so scared he didn't know what to do. He knew there was a time in every boy's life when they became a man, when puberty caused their bodies to change. Now his body was changing. He could feel it, bones grinding painfully as they shifted into new configurations that would be better suited for survival.

He was sad that his mom and sisters couldn't change like him, that he had eaten them. But he was grateful; he knew without their sustenance, he wouldn't have had the energy he needed to grow. Puberty was not what he had expected, but it had come, and now the world looked and smelled differently. The pain was ebbing, and he could smell the acrid stench of his family in the other room. Should he eat more? He should, but he was still scared.

He swung his head up and down, trying to get his loose

skin out of his eyes, before growing too frustrated. He screamed a multi-chordal scream that filled the small bathroom and was echoed by answering screams from outside the cramped apartment. He reached up and grabbed his loose face flesh in his claws. He ripped and tore at the skin, peeling it from his skull, and he shredded his flesh. The tendons and connective tissue tried to stay attached, but he shredded it, heedless of the damage he did to his nerves and muscles. In the end, his face fell into the sink beneath him.

His skinless skull, rife with bleeding muscles that twitched, stared down at his flaccid face. Sorrow and fear filled him. He didn't want to be a man; he wasn't ready to be a grownup. He needed his mommy.

She's dead and gone.

She's food. Eat.

She's Mommy, and I need her and can't have her.

You can have her inside you.

Gil screamed again as his thoughts warred within him. But he knew he could never be comforted by his mother again. But that didn't mean all hope was lost. Papa. Papa had been here before the bad man had hurt him. Papa was a man; he had gone through puberty; he had done this already. Papa could help.

Gil's head swam pleasantly as he realized all he needed to do was find his papa and everything would be all right again. Papa could protect him. With this in mind, Gil leapt off the edge of the sink, blissfully numb to the pain of both his wound and the rapid evolution of his body. He had a plan. He inhaled deeply. The muscles surrounding his bloody nostrils—now little more than simple olfactory holes—flexed, and he caught the familiar scent of aftershave, gunpowder, and cheaply made cigarettes. There was the scent; there was Papa.

He craned his neck to peer around the small apartment he had called home. There was safety here, food. Every bit of common sense told him this was where he should stay;

he was safe here among the familiar scents and sights of his nest. But Papa's smell beckoned him, called to him. Gilberto scuttled out the door. Before, he had always found the flickering bulbs and the deep shadows of the apartment hallways claustrophobic and terrifying. Who knew what was hiding in those deep corners of blackness? Now, the shadows were comforting, places where he could hide and, if need be, ambush any smaller prey that came by. Again tempting, but the biological meat of his brain that still clung to the tattered remains of synapses that could just barely be called human screamed at him that he needed his daddy.

He crawled low across the hall, pausing at each door to sniff. He was moving slowly. The sheer information overload of a world of scent-markers and strange inorganic smells was almost too much for his adolescent brain to handle. He moved methodically, sniffing along the wall, his skinless face pressed to the ground as he snorted in. As he passed the doors in the halls, he could hear the sounds of other people. Some of them were going through puberty like him; others were sobbing and screaming.

This was Abuela Maria's door. He sniffed deeply; he could smell her fresh baking through the door, but he could also hear her gurgles and something else tearing at flesh. He didn't need to use his imagination to understand what was happening. His sister had made the same noise. Then next was his friend Rigoberto; Rig and Gil, they were a known mischievous duo in the complex—or had been. Gil couldn't hear anything through the door, but he knew that if he could come across someone Rig's size, that would absolutely be prey that he could overcome.

At each door, Gil considered his neighbors, if they were alive or dead, if they were changing like him, and if they would make good prey. In the end, though, he knew he was only postponing what he was actually fearing. The front doors of the complex, the wide world out there. He wondered if Papa would be just outside those doors. Maybe he would be; maybe he would be right there ready to hold Gil and teach him how to hunt, teach him how to take down larger prey. It was all he could think about. He needed to hunt, he needed to kill and eat more, but most of all, he needed his daddy.

With that in mind, he pushed away from the shadows of the wall and loped towards the front doors. It was like pulling off a band-aid, he thought, or a face; the faster he got it over with, the less it would hurt, the less fear would have time to interfere with him, to convince him he should just hide back in his home.

He pushed through the door and was assaulted by the daylight outside. It was an orange, sickly sunlight colored by the smoke that rose over the burning city, but it was brighter than it had been inside. The world was an insane scramble of colors and smells that offered every experience a 12-year-old boy could ever want. Every taste, every smell.

It took him several moments to pick out Papa's smell from the swirling chaos of chemicals in the air. It would be easy to get distracted, but he wanted his daddy; he wanted that, and food, and . . . something else, something he had never wanted before, something he couldn't quite wrap his slowly crumbling psyche around. But he wanted it, and it wasn't in the apartments behind him; it was out here in the world. His eyes, unhindered by flesh, were wide with wonder at the world of scents and sounds that greeted him as he left the complex.

9.

IL WAS RIGHT. The world outside his nest was terrifying. He was small enough that he could pull himself under the cars that sat on the road if he needed to find shelter and safety, but many of them were engulfed in flames, scorchingly hot to even approach. But conversely, the smoke that filled the air meant that the sky wasn't visible and he wasn't visible to whatever predators were above. And he could hear them, even if he couldn't see or smell them, the keening cry that sounded like something between a woman's wail and a cicada's buzzing chirp. Gil wondered what the flying predator would look like. He wondered if he was akin to the wingless beetle-things that crawled from the ground, and if he would harden and then emerge as a flying creature too.

The idea of flight was very appealing to Gilberto. He had always been a fan of superheroes and science-fiction. The idea of the freedom of flight, especially for a poor boy growing up in what amounted to barrio housing, it seemed like paradise on Earth. To be able to look up into the sky and go anywhere, do anything, was his greatest fantasy. But now it had practicality to it as well. If he could fly, he would be able to follow Papa's scent without worrying about terrestrial predators. He would also be able to find things like water and prey for his own consumption.

But he didn't have wings. Perhaps one day he would grow them. Though, did people grow wings? Could little boys grow extra fingers? Gilberto raised his hand to his face, sniffing at the extra digits. The part of him that was human screamed and bucked against the terror of his changing body. He knew that whatever it was above the clouds of smoke hunting him, it wasn't human any more than he was. And that knowledge terrified him.

A scream pulled him from his existential terror with its own—it wasn't one of existential loathing but of visceral and vital panic. There were people. Gilberto turned his attention to the group of people running down the street. They had emerged from a side street and turned away from him in their mad dash. Before he could consider this development, Gil was charging after them, the predator instinct triggered by the prey running. He watched them as they ran, knowing they were running from some other predator. But there were so many, surely even another predator wouldn't mind his encroachment. He watched the perimeter of the panicked herd of people. No matter how much they wanted to protect each other and not leave anyone behind, the elderly, the young, and the sickly all got pushed to the edges by the healthy mass of the writhing horde of flesh.

Gil considered a large female that was near the back edge of the herd. It was huffing and puffing. She was a deliriously attractive target, she would be easy to take down and comprised plenty of meat to fill his belly. The creature chasing the people emerged from the side street, hot on the heels of the humans and just ahead of Gilberto. It was tremendously large, an insane amalgamation of scything limbs and snapping jaws. It wailed a jarring dirge of hunger and violence as it charged the fleeing people.

Gil followed, loping into the street after them. His tongue lolled out of his mouth as he ran, long and covered in hook-like growths, perfect for snagging prey and dragging it into his waiting gullet. He was no longer in any pain, but instead of the world slowing down and spinning like it usually did when he took Papa's medicine, everything seemed to be clearer than it ever was. He could taste the acrid scent of sweat and fear coming off the runners. It was mouthwatering. He continued to chase, constantly mindful of the position of the larger predator—he did not want to be mistaken for one of the prey animals.

Prey animals?

Those were people. He thought he even recognized Mr. Estaben from the mercado down the street. Those were people, just like him. But they were running. They were running, and if he didn't eat, he wouldn't have enough energy to find Papa. And if he didn't have energy, he would become prey himself. Maybe even Mr. Estaben would eat him if he wasn't able to protect himself! Gil couldn't let that happen. He looked ahead; there were more things, people like him, changed, adapting, growing. The unchanged people were running right for them. They would be trapped. He slowed down, letting the larger hunters do the work for him.

The people realized the terrible danger they were in too late. Those at the front of the herd tried to halt their flight towards the waiting ambush, they tried to change direction, but the press of panicked bodies behind them carried them forward. Right into the drooling, snapping jaws ahead. The smell of blood and torn flesh filled Gil's nostrils. He couldn't help himself; he threw his head back and let out a screeching scream-like howl. Those creatures not actively engaged in tearing flesh from the ribs and faces of their prey answered him—a chorus of discordant hymns rising to the heavens in absolute adulation for the hunt and meals, grace sung around the table of slaughter.

Gil sprang forward, tackling a slender girl who had become separated from her father and pushed to the outskirts of the herd. She screamed, her face inches from his. He screamed back, phlegm and blood splattering against her cheek as he pressed her face into the rough asphalt. Did he know her? Was she familiar to him? He realized he couldn't tell.

He looked up from his prize, at the other people; they

were a mass of screaming, writhing stink. He could only distinguish them between those who had already been torn apart by the predators and those that still struggled to get free and escape—fewer of those latter with every passing second as the massive creature that had been chasing them waded into the sea of terrified faces and began reaping them with each swing of its blade-like limbs.

She was a people. He knew this in his heart, but as Gil looked down, he couldn't tell her apart from any other people. He couldn't see anything other than prey, food to be consumed, a possible threat to be eliminated. She was still screaming. He wasn't too concerned about her bringing others to her aid; everyone that could help her was either dead and torn apart or would soon join the mass of meat. Some part of him was screaming that he needed to find his papa, that he couldn't waste his time devouring this girl, this child his own age. She was like him.

But she wasn't like him, not anymore. He was more; he was different, better. More evolved to survive and to attain the necessary resources to stay alive. He tilted his head, craning his neck in twitching movements to look around and ensure that none of the other predators were taking interest in him. Those that were not actively hunting and devouring their own catches were doing the same as him. An uneasy truce—there was plenty of food for the group of changed; they didn't need to compete, not for now.

Gilberto lowered his face to the screaming girl, impressed that she still had voice in her lungs while he crouched on her chest. His bulbous eyes stayed on the largest of the fellow predators as he sank his teeth into the cheek of the girl, ripping up with a jerk to tear her face meat free. Her screams became squeals of terror as he worked his jaws over the skin and muscle tissue he had gotten free. He chewed for a second, listening to her sounds as the shock overtook her, taking her from full-throated yelping to horrid mewling. Gulping down his prize, Gilberto leaned forward and punched his tongue into the girl's eye socket, curling around the orb and yanking it free. He rolled it in his mouth for a moment before crushing it and slurping the juices down eagerly. It was transcendently delicious. He wanted more. Gil leaned down, jamming his tongue into the empty socket once more, using the rough texture that had grown on the muscle to tear and pull any organic matter he could free from her skull and into his waiting mouth.

Her struggling finally fell still as his tongue punctured the blood brain barrier, and he used his long prehensile tongue to drag a chunk of cranial meat through her eye and into his gullet. As he emptied the little girl's skull, all thoughts of his father, of what he was, of humanity itself disappeared into the void of what he had become.

FORGIVENESS

R. SANCHEZ'S EXPERIENCE was far from unique. All across the world, people were forced to abandon or fight off their afflicted family members. Humanity reached out to their supposed saviors only to find the gates were barred and the draw bridges had been raised. It was no surprise, really; we had seen the same thing anytime there was an oppressed group. We help others when it is convenient to do so. Altruism existed as a critically endangered animal lost in a sea of poachers. When one does try to help, they are inundated by scam artists and conmen waiting to take advantage of any scrap of kindness they can to gain more. Or else those who claim your acts are not altruistic or are benefiting the wrong group. No good deed goes unpunished by the court of popular opinion. We are creatures born of greed and little else.

Of course, in hindsight, we still

don't know if there is any "cure," any way to reverse the horrific changes wrought by the Abhorrence. And even if we could return someone's psyche, make them think like humans again, could a human mind truly comprehend the horror of what had become of their body? I think it may be the sole solace of the afflicted that they have no human understanding of what they are or what they are becoming. Other than a few anomalies like King, none of the afflicted ever seem to hold on to anything human. Not that we can tell. I pray they don't.

Prayer . . .

It's amazing to me that religion has survived at all after the Abhorrence, or perhaps it isn't that strange. Mr. Sanchez admitted that he thought the afflicted were demon-possessed. That's certainly what monsters like Aiden King preached. And so religion remains in place. Prayers continue to ascend to the empty throne of a god who couldn't possibly exist in the same reality in which the Abhorrence took place.

But I understand; people need comfort, they need answers, even if those answers don't actually address the root causes and catastrophes that have taken place. I would be hard-

ABHORRENT ACCORDS

pressed to answer to the greater evil:
man's creations or creation's men.

Alexander Fienkolt
University of Texas, Archivist

PART 3:

PROPHET

HENEVER THERE IS a tragedy, we want to pin the blame on someone, something. So many of us chose to blame the cartels. Hardly anyone considers the systems in place in global pharmaceuticals and the logistical nightmare that only our governments could have built in order to get the tainted products to every corner of the world. If pharma companies hadn't leapt at the chance for cheaper morphine and fentanyl, would the carnage have been contained to Central America?

As much as we want to find the villain, there are no innocents in the Abhorrence. Within the Emergence, all of us are abhorrent.

Even still, it's difficult not to look towards the figure of Aiden King as the worst of the villains. The entirety of his part in all of this will probably never really be known. Just like we don't really know much about his past, only that he emerged from San Antonio, a "survivor" who came preaching comforting words of peace and kindness to embed himself in communities heading north, seemingly

always just ahead of the ravening
horde of the afflicted.

What we do know of Aiden King we
have gleaned from the few survivors
that have been left in his bloody wake
and from the scattered recordings of
his sermons recovered from the scenes
of massacres.

Alexander Fienkolt
University of Texas, Archivist

A WOLF ENTERS

SHEPPARD AIR FORCE BASE
THE GOSPEL OF RYAN BRADLEY

IO.

S AN ANTONIO WAS LOST—hell, so was Austin—and it looked like the monster, the big one, was heading towards Dallas. Ryan sat on the cot provided him by the soldiers, his arm looped around his daughter. Two months ago seemed like a lifetime. He hadn't been important or wealthy, but he had had everything he needed. A good wife, a wonderful daughter (even if the teen attitude was hitting hard), a job, and a house. Then . . . then the Abhorrent came clawing its way out of hell and set the world on fire. Of course, Ryan had no idea there was a giant monster—a kaiju or whatever they were called—destroying south Texas when he took his family and fled from his home.

Then it was just the so-called afflicted. And holy shit, there had been a lot of them. Too many of them. Ryan closed his eyes, trying to physically block out the memory of the creature that had broken the window and dragged his wife away. He had already spent weeks trying to convince himself that it wasn't his fault. But the pain and the guilt showed no signs of abating. All he could do was try to be strong for Sam; she had lost her mother, her friends, her entire life was gone in a flash, something no sixteen-year-old girl should have to endure. But endure it she would; there was no other choice, no other options.

Ryan felt lost. His wife was ripped from his life so quickly, so completely, and there had been no time to mourn until they reached Sheppard Air Force Base. Even

76

then, and now, he felt he couldn't let his guard down, couldn't take the time to feel sad, to be vulnerable. He needed to be strong for Sam, not just emotionally but physically. She wasn't a little girl anymore, and he could see that so many of the men on the base were ready to look at her—and treat her—like a woman. She didn't need that. She needed her father to step up and protect her, and goddamnit, he would do exactly that.

"Hey, Mr. Bradley, Sam."

His thoughts were interrupted by Joey Garcia, a kid about Sam's age. He was a nice enough boy, seemed respectful, but Ryan had been around long enough to be able to spot the signs of infatuation that the kid had towards his daughter. Fine, as long as they stayed feelings and not actions.

"What is it, Joey?" he asked, not eager to try to pull himself out of the funk he was feeling.

"There's a newcomer . . . just came through the gate last night," Joey said, nearly buzzing with excitement at the news.

Ryan stared at the kid before glancing down at Sam to see if she cared. She looked up at him and then glanced at Joey before lowering her eyes once again. Seeing his normally outgoing, extroverted daughter retreat once more into her shell was almost enough to break his heart all over again. Joey was on civilian door duty, meaning that whenever the soldiers were stretched too thin—or didn't feel like doing their fucking jobs—Joey would stand watch at the gates for any survivors or any sign of afflicted that could fly and therefore wouldn't be slowed by the gate.

"People come in all the time, Joey, another mouth to feed, another stretch on resources," Sam whispered.

"Yeah, but this one, this guy, he's a preacher!"

Ryan blinked; well that was different. Before the afflicted things had come, Ryan, Sam, and Melissa had gone to church every Sunday. Ryan wouldn't call his family extremely religious, but he liked being a good Christian man. It felt good instilling Christian values in Sam. And preachers and priests were some of the first who fell to the afflicted, who seemed to crawl out of those cesspits that clergy would tend to. Like a poisonous garden that had finally risen up to devour its gardener. But for a preacher to have survived outside the walls of a compound or fortified community for this long, that was nothing short of miraculous.

"You're sure?" Ryan asked.

"Yeah, he called himself Reverend King. Said he had been running since he left San Antonio!" Joey whispered that. They had all heard what happened in San Antonio; they had all seen the news feed before the airwaves had gone dead. The Abhorrent, a massive monster that tore the heart out of the city and spread the affliction with its every step.

"No . . . that ain't possible," Ryan said, more to himself.

"Unless . . . " Joey suggested.

"Unless it was a miracle," Ryan finished.

II.

SHEPPARD AIR FORCE BASE
SERMON OF REVEREND KING

FRIENDS, I AM just so blessed to be here today. So blessed to be able to stand before you. Amen! Every day after San Antonio, after that demon came, I have asked and begged God, "Why, oh Jesus, why? Why was I spared? Why was I alone allowed to flee and survive?" It's so I could come here! You are safe from the monsters here, but are you safe from the Devil? Are you safe from Satan?

Not without church. Not without guidance from Jesus. And so here I am.

Friend, brothers, sisters. I have listened to the radio transmissions that are coming through. I have been paying attention. And God have mercy, you see what is happening, right? They are trying to ask the scientists, but the scientists have no answers! This ain't nothing new. Because we all know there's only one answer out there, right?

Jesus! That's right. The Lamb of God is the only answer, and the absence of Jesus is what leads to this. Friends, we have to. We have to stick together through all of this. We have to have each other's backs, and not just on watch; no, we have to have each other's backs spiritually. When you see your friend, when you see your family deciding, "Hey I don't need to go pray today. There's no point in saying grace," boy, you just gotta get to them and talk some sense into them.

Part of being Christian, part of being godly, is

recognizing we don't have power, we don't have strength outside of Jesus, outside of God the Father. So anytime you, or anyone else, tried to go alone and put God to the side, well you already lost that battle. Look at Jesus on the cross, right? Jesus said, "My God, why have you forsaken me?" Those were the last words of Jesus. Everyone wants to point out this loving "forgive them for they know not what they do," but the truth is that in those moments, Jesus lost his faith in God.

(Wait for murmurs and shock to die down)

And then he died. And THEN he died! Think about that. The son of God! He loses his faith for a second, just a moment, and he dies! Think about that. We all excuse lack of faith, lack of Christian morals and actions, saying, "Oh, it's understandable under the circumstances." Is it? Is it understandable that you've been through a lot and so God should forgive you? That God should forgive you sinning or looking the other way as others sin? You think that's what a loving god would do? How much more love do you need than eternal life and paradise? How much more grace do y'all need? Think about it. A momentary lapse during intense torture and punishment from the Romans, and the son of God lost his fight. You can't win a fight without God; you can't win a fight without Jesus.

Friends, we are all here for a purpose. We are all here to make things better. Because that's what being Christian is about. It's about improving this world and living as close to Jesus's example as we possibly can. That means being good, that means being kind to your fellow Christian, and it means surviving to carry on Jesus's message. We all know how fragile life can be, how hard; we have all seen the face of Satan himself in these afflicted, and it IS Satan, I can promise you that. The only way out of this mess is through acts of Christian goodness. It's the only way to survive, both in body and, more importantly, in soul.

12.

RYAN WAS ENERGIZED by the sermon. That was the sort of thing he liked most, when preachers spoke about hope. Not that Reverend King had specifically said the word hope. But that was the message, wasn't it? That through Christian acts, there was hope? He had also never heard a preacher say that Jesus had failed in anything before. It had sent a shock through his system, making him feel like he was awake and alive for the first time since getting to this damn airbase.

The reverend had wasted no time in getting set up on the base, moving into the chapel and organizing a Sunday service. Not too many people had shown up for that first service. Ryan wasn't surprised, even if he was disappointed. Maybe the news hadn't spread that there would be a service. Or maybe, Ryan thought, maybe people were just like Jesus up on that cross, a second away from species wide extinction and they had lost whatever faith they had in their hearts. People said there were no such things as atheists in foxholes.

But from what Ryan saw, only the most religiously devout still carried God in their hearts, and really, it seemed like only the Jews and the Muslims were really holding on, at least in his opinion. But now there was a reverend on base! There would be services, sermons, community. And maybe a home for God on the base would help Sam come out of her shell.

He stood next to the big chain link fence on the

outskirts of the base, the only thing that really separated them from the monsters on the other side of the fence. Well the only physical barrier. The wall was patrolled 24/7 by no less than ten pairs of guards constantly circling, fully automatic weapons at the ready. Of course, keeping that sort of precaution meant that the base needed to rely on more than just airmen, and able-bodied refugees were pressed into service as well, like Ryan.

Not that Ryan minded, it gave him a sense of purpose; it helped him feel like he was actually doing something, contributing something. And every single afflicted that he gunned down was another chance to seek absolution for his wife's death. Out there, in the world, life was ending. Apocalypse, Armageddon, whatever you wanted to call it, it was the end of everything as they had known it.

The stench of rot and sickness was almost overpowering near the wall. Ryan, like all guards, wore a painter's ventilation mask to minimize the stink that wafted from the decaying corpses just on the other side of the mesh fence. They had tried digging mass graves and burning the bodies at first, but the smoke and noise attracted more of the afflicted. So now, the dead—monstrous and human alike—rotted, baking in the North Texas sun. It was the worst when the wind blew the stench into the base.

Ryan turned to look at the piles of bones and sun-parched flesh that stretched between rotting limbs. He couldn't have imagined a more gruesome hell if he had tried.

"Terrible, isn't it?" a voice said from behind Ryan.

He turned quickly and was surprised to see Reverend King standing there.

"Hey, Reverend!" Ryan glanced back at the desolation of the world beyond their fences. "Yeah. Terrible. Makes you question, well, everything, really."

"Everything? Ah, you're talking about my sermon, aren't you? Well. Yes, everyone questions. The truth is that if even Jesus can doubt, what hope do we have?" The Reverend clapped a hand on Ryan's shoulder. It radiated cold and left a wet mark on Ryan's shirt. But he was too distracted by how strong the pat was, how much power the reverend seemed to pack in his arm.

"I guess not much," Ryan said

"Ah, that's where you're wrong, Mr. . . . ."

"Bradley, sir, Ryan C. Bradley."

"Mr. Bradley." King smiled, and for a moment, it looked unnatural, like he had far more teeth in his mouth than he should. Ryan shook the image out of his head; he had been cooped up staring at monsters for so long he was seeing them everywhere. "See, we may not have much hope of going on without any shadow of doubt crossing the threshold, but we have constant and sure hope in Jesus's sacrifice for us. Remember that, brother Bradley."

King stepped past him, almost to the fence. Ryan was about to warn him that it was electrified, but the pastor didn't make any move to touch the metal, his watery blue eyes seeming unfocused, pointed towards the horizon.

"It's out there, the Abhorrent," King whispered.

"You said you came from San Antonio, Reverend? How did you escape?" It was the obvious question but not the one he wanted to ask.

"Oh, same way you escaped . . . wherever you came from. With the grace of God on my lips and the wind of the divine on my back."

"You saw it?"

There it was; that was what everyone wanted to know. Had he seen the Abhorrent? While they had all seen and survived afflicted attacks, the reports from South Texas of a massive monster that towered above cities and brought an army of afflicted with it kept them up at night. Their defenses were nothing next to a creature that could crush buildings. Their electric fence and guns wouldn't do shit if the creature's presence caused affliction. As long as the threat was human sized and bled, it could be dealt with.

But from what the soldiers at the base said, the Army had thrown everything it had at the monster, and it hadn't even slowed down. Ryan, like every civilian on the base, wanted the truth; he wanted comfort that something like that wasn't real.

"Oh yes," King said, his face contorting with unidentifiable emotion at the memory of coming face to face with the creature. "I wonder if it's what Moses felt when he came face to face with God. Something so much more than natural, proof of God, of Satan, of it all."

"Is it . . . as terrible as they say?" Ryan asked, a fearful whisper that barely rose above the North Texas wind.

"More," Reverend King said with a sigh. "Understand that as humans, it is not meant for us to comprehend the full might of the adversary. We can see God through the words of the Bible, and we see Satan in the face of the addict, the whore, the thief. That's how we are supposed to understand evil. We aren't meant to look evil in its literal eyes. But that's what we do; that's where we are."

"Evil? The doctors on base say that the majority of the affliction is passed through morphine."

"Morphine, heroin, drugs. Brother Bradley. What more proof do you need? A drug that is meant to help but that evil men become addicted to and peddle for money, a substance women trade their bodies for. What better symbol of evil could you ask for? The faces of the drug addicts and whores twist to reveal their inner nature. Even good Christians polluted with the poison fall to the archenemy." The reverend sighed and shrugged; he looked conflicted about his own words, though Ryan couldn't begin to guess why.

"But I didn't come here to talk doom and gloom, brother Bradley! I noticed you in the chapel; thank you for coming to the service."

"My pleasure—" Ryan started, but the reverend lifted his hand to cut him off.

"I noticed a young woman with you," King said.

"Oh, well yes, that's my daughter." Suddenly, Ryan felt defensive, then immediately felt guilty for feeling defensive. He needed to trust someone, and who could he trust more than a preacher? "Sam."

"Sam?" King's eyebrow raised.

"Samantha," Ryan clarified.

"Oh, good, I was worried she was one of those tomboys or, worse, one of those trans. Less of those wandering around now."

Ryan shuffled a little. He knew that sort of talk would get someone in hot water before the Emergence; hell, it would land him in hot water with Sam if she heard it. But she wasn't around, and he didn't want to cross the reverend. "Uh, no, sir, she just goes by Sam for short. She's a good kid, just turned sixteen before the . . . " He trailed off, not wanting to think about the trauma they had gone through since her birthday.

"Sixteen," King said, his watery eyes bright with excitement. "Well, as you know, I'm coming in here, I'm trying to—I hate to say set up shop, but I'm trying to make sure Christ has a home in this base, and part of that is ministering to the youth. Youth like Samantha. I would like it if you would bring her to me, to the chapel, I mean. I think she could do great work for the Lord and for Jesus by spreading the good news to others. Any good youth group starts with a strong and charismatic leader. Do you think you and Sam could help me help Jesus?"

13.

SAM SAT IN the cafeteria watching the group of soldiers across the mess hall. Next to her, Rebecca sat poking at her own food without much interest. It had become a ritual. Whenever her dad was on patrol, she would come and eat. But always with a friend. Never alone. She had learned that not all of the monsters were on the other side of the fence. When men thought they could get away with it, they would be as terrifying and dangerous as any of the afflicted. Even with Rebecca by her side, Sam didn't feel entirely comfortable. So she always watched the men to see where they were, what they were doing, if they were getting too close.

"So, youth group," Rebecca said, pulling Sam's attention away from her vigil.

"Youth group," Sam agreed. "I don't know; it seems stupid to me. I feel like we have more important stuff to deal with than a book written two thousand years ago."

"I don't know, my mom is pretty adamant about me studying my bible. She says it's the only way Jews have survived stuff like this. As if stuff like this ever happened before."

"I feel like if we would stop paying attention to what a bunch of dead people wrote, maybe we would be better off." Sam sighed. "Like, how is knowing the names of the twelve apostles supposed to help us against the afflicted?"

"I don't know. I don't think pacifism is a winning choice. Do you even believe in God?" Rebecca asked.

ABHORRENT ACCORDS

Sam didn't answer immediately, rolling the question around on her tongue. Her parents had always dragged her to church, and as a small child, she had been unwaveringly faithful to the beliefs of her father. But when she got to high school and was confronted by people who absolutely did not believe in God, who didn't believe in Jesus, she began to question. After all, what sort of God allowed war? What sort of God would champion preachers who screamed hatred towards queer folk while they themselves molested children? Those were questions she didn't dare ask her parents, and so she had sat with them in silence.

"No," Sam finally answered. "I don't think that any sort of loving God could create a world like this. If there is a God, they aren't worth worshiping. Sorry."

"It doesn't bother me," Rebecca admitted. "I think I believe in God, but who knows, I guess I'm more agnostic than anything. The Jewish stuff, it's culture, it's tradition, but a lot of the time, I just feel like I'm going through the motions to keep good with my parents."

"Yeah. Same. I'm supposed to do this youth group thing now, outreach to other kids. I don't know how I'm supposed to convince other people to join this church when I don't want to be there myself. Most people here just want to be left alone; it's all any of us want, I think."

"You're getting so gloomy," Rebecca said with a smile. "You still have your friends, and this youth group stuff is just like any other religious thing: play along, keep everyone happy. Eventually, it won't matter. If this whole shit show has proven anything, it's that people need to worry about what's actually happening, not what other people are doing in the privacy of their own homes and hearts."

Sam smiled; Rebecca had a point. After all, what was the point in rocking the boat? Her dad wasn't handling the loss of her mom very well, and this church stuff obviously meant a lot to him. She could handle some lip service to a god that wouldn't answer back. Even if Reverend King gave her the creeps. "Yeah, you're right."

"Usually am!" Rebecca said with a grin, finishing the last of her MRE. "But, that's the burden of being me. And your burden for being my friend. So what does youth group actually mean? Like, what do you have to do?"

Sam was about to answer when a loud discordant scream filled the air. Everyone, from the girls to the soldiers sitting across the hall to the staff working in the cafeteria, froze. No one had gotten there unscathed. Everyone at the base held their breath, waiting for the sound of screams and terror, just waiting for that moment when the world exploded into chaos. But instead of screams and terror, the sound of large caliber rifles being fired echoed across the base. And then silence. After a moment, a loud tone issued from the PA system, the all clear, letting the inhabitants of the base know that the immediate threat of the afflicted was neutralized.

Sam and Rebecca fell into silence as Sam finished her food. They no longer felt like talking about the youth group, or anything else, really. What was the point of looking towards heaven when they were already sentenced to hell?

14.

SHEPPARD AIR FORCE BASE
SERMON OF REVEREND KING

OH LORD, hear my prayers here and now. We ask that you protect us. I pray that we benefit from your sword arm to strike down our enemies even as we make peace with yours.

You all hear that, right? You hear the lunacy of what I just asked? I asked God to do for us what we are unwilling to do for him! What do we call that, when we ask and ask and ask and don't give back? Don't worry, it's rhetorical; we both know what it's called. Hypocrisy! It's called playing games with the Lord, and if you think that God is playing games, well you sure as HELL ain't paying attention. Look outside! Look outside the gates of this blessed base—which, by the way, the godless demon-rats, they tried to defund this. You think that's a coincidence? You think that our safety coming from the Army of America DESPITE what the liberals tried to do is a coincidence?

God, let them see, open their eyes to the truth. You think God is playing games, that God is going to flip a switch somewhere and turn off the End Times? That ain't how it works, not in any iteration of the good book. If you open your bibles, if you take a long look at what God himself said, you know that this is just the beginning. Now, some of y'all are getting angry; some of y'all don't like that I come up here and tell the truth. Some of you get pissed that I'm making God out to be some cruel figure who doesn't love and need us.

But that's the truth. The damned truth, literally. God doesn't need us. God isn't powered by our prayers and belief. God is all mighty, all powerful, and all knowing. God isn't some hard-up punk looking for friends. We don't worship God for God's sake but for ours, and it's the definition of hubris to assume we have the power in that relationship, that we think we can decide what God wants without deferring to the Gospels!

You think that you can second-guess that? That you can reinterpret the Bible to make it sound like homosexuality isn't a sin? Like the trans agenda isn't a satanic cabal set to infect the world with mental illness? You think you get to ignore the Bible and then ask why God is ignoring you? You think I haven't seen the jokes? That if you don't sin, then Jesus died for nothing? You think that it's a joke?

Lord Jesus, help me explain to these people, you don't get to be good people and also ignore bad things. You don't get into Heaven when you loop your arms around Satan and say it's in the name of love.

When Jesus said let him without sin cast the first stone, he didn't mean you should embrace the sinner and their sin as your own. What he meant is you should be pure and either distance yourself from the heathen, the pagan, and the sinner OR bring them to his house.

Think about that phrase, friends; think about how this is Jesus's house. The entire universe belongs to God, but the world, well, that belongs to Satan. This world was given to Satan to tempt us and lead us astray. The only safe haven is here, in Jesus's house. It's like we're playing tag and this is the base. Now I'm not saying we have to drive the Muslims and Jews out of the base; I understand what situation we are in. But I am saying that the situation we are in doesn't excuse us from doing the work, from bringing the misguided to Jesus to welcome them into the house.

ABHORRENT ACCORDS

I look up and I see your faces. I see more of you in here each week. And that's great. But the heart of the church is outreach, and Jesus is insatiable. He doesn't just want us; he wants everyone on this base to know him.

The end is on us, and anyone who denies that, well, they are Satan's mouthpiece. The only hope now is to drag as many people into Jesus's arms as possible, to save as many souls and make ready for the King of kings to bless us all with his presence.

THE FOURTH SEAL

SHEPPARD AIR FORCE BASE —THE COMING BEAST

15.

SAM SAT IN the stairwell of one of the towers, looking down at the student's study bible that her dad had packed for her. Of course, "for her" didn't mean much at all. The more time she spent in the Reverend King's presence, the more she heard his hateful spiel, the less she believed in any god. Maybe Jesus was real, maybe God was, but if any word about Jesus made sense, then Christianity didn't. Sam sighed and set the bible down on the stairs beside her. The worst thing was her dad was swallowing all of the shit that King was shoveling. It was like he was taking the hole in his heart that her mom's death had left and was trying to fill it with whatever he could find.

She couldn't blame him, or hate him. But she was angry. He was always a kind person, or at least she had thought he was. More and more lately, he was letting King's cruelty infect him. Maybe her mom had been the only thing holding her dad in check, or maybe he was just a weak man who clung to whoever had authority near him. How different would things be here in the base if her mom had made it? Sam couldn't help but think she would have either walked out of King's bullshit sermons or else confronted the bigot herself.

Sam sniffed, keeping her tears back through sheer angry will.

"Sam?" It was her dad.

Sam sighed, closing her eyes. She had come here to be

alone but knew it would be worse for her, and for her dad, if she hid from him.

"I'm here," she called back.

"Hey, cupcake," Ryan said as he pulled up the stairs and came to a stop in front of her. "Oh, honey." He sighed when he saw the tears she was so clearly fighting. People no longer asked others what was wrong when they saw tears. The question had become meaningless in a world where everything was terrible. "Mom?" he asked instead.

Sam nodded, even if it was only half the reason she was crying, even if her tears were angrier than they were sad. The truth was that grief had lost its weight in this place. One could only be sad for so long before it slipped from grief to depression. And Sam was too fucking angry to be depressed. She didn't blame her dad for her mom's death, but she was angry at him all the same. She was angry that they survived when her mom died. She was angry that they came to this place and were living like refugees just waiting to be overwhelmed by the afflicted, just waiting for death. And if all that wasn't enough, now she had to be subjected to the same hateful version of Christianity she had hoped had been butchered by the Emergence.

"Reverend King said you missed youth group," Ryan said as he sat down next to her on the stairs. "I just wanted to check on you, make sure you were okay."

"I don't want to do youth group," Sam said simply. She immediately felt her father tense next to her.

"Sam . . . " Ryan began.

"I don't want to," she repeated.

Ryan nodded and rubbed her shoulder. "Now is not the time to let your faith in God waver, and your part in building a good Christian community here, it's super important. Lots of people don't know Jesus; they've never had the opportunity."

"Dad, I don't . . . " She stopped before she admitted to not believing in Jesus or God or anything. "I don't like Reverend King; he creeps me out."

"Samantha!" Ryan hissed sharply. "Reverend King is a good man. He's speaking the word of God and trying to bring people together. He's just older and passionate about God." The truth was that Ryan was in awe of the reverend. In a few short weeks, he had become the leader of the Christians in the camp, growing the small congregation until it hardly fit in the chapel. It seemed almost everyone on the base was attending the reverend's sermons.

"He's an old racist," Sam pressed.

"Damnit, Samantha." Ryan stood. "I know you're hurting and angry, but you don't take that shit out on the preacher. Just because he's saying things you don't like to hear don't mean that they aren't true or that he's a bad person."

"He said that Jews and Muslims are the enemy, Dad; that's racist."

"No, Samantha, he didn't mean that they are enemies; he means that they are misguided. He means that it's our job as Christians to introduce them to a relationship with Christ. And he's absolutely right; that's what we're supposed to be doing. That's our job."

"Why is it our job? Why does it matter what people believe or worship when the world is already hell?" Sam was aware she was getting louder, but she didn't care. She didn't want to be forced to fake smile and be around that preacher.

"Don't you say that. This world is all we have, and Reverend King says that the only solace we have is that we get to go to Heaven. Do you get that? Your mother was a good Christian, and if we're good Christians, we get to be with her forever."

"When we die, Dad, if any of this stuff is real; it doesn't matter until we die. We aren't dead now. We are alive, and we have to live, and we have to survive. Mom was never okay with bigots; she wouldn't want you clinging to that guy like this! And we shouldn't even be going to his sermons; it's a waste of time! The Abhorrent is coming. I heard the soldiers talking about it. We should be looking for a way out, a way to escape and survive, not wasting our time with this . . . asshole!"

Ryan raised his hand. He wanted to slap her. He wanted to stop her accusations. But he didn't have the strength. It made him feel weak; he couldn't even be a strong father. He hadn't been strong enough to keep his wife, the love of his life, alive. Now he couldn't be strong enough to discipline his own daughter. He stared at her, wanting to intimidate her, wanting her to recognize his role as the decision-maker, the man of the family. Sam, for her part, met his eyes with a fierce willpower so reminiscent of her mom that it forced Ryan to break and look away.

"I have to go report in for watch," he lied. "But we're not done with this conversation, Samantha. Not by a long shot." He watched her, hoping she would show some sign of contrition, or at least the sort of submissiveness that a parent was supposed to be shown. Nothing. There was usually at least some sign of respect in her eyes, but today, right now, there was only anger. Ryan held his head up as high as he could muster and retreated down the stairs, unwilling to give voice to the defeat he was feeling.

16.

SHEPPARD AIR FORCE BASE
SERMON OF REVEREND KING

THERE'S THIS SAYING calling Jews the chosen ones. Chosen for what? Well, I spoke to a Rabbi in San Antonio right before it was destroyed. That's right; while the world was going to hell, I was out there trying to bring the misguided to Jesus. But that's not the point yet; the point is that they believe they were chosen to bring their version of the Holy Bible to the world. Can you imagine?

They believe they were chosen to be God's special children. No, the Jews were chosen to be the people from which Jesus came. Can you imagine your entire purpose is to usher in the son of God, to welcome in grace and forgiveness to human kind? And then you reject it? Not only do you reject it, you assassinate the son of God, you go out of your way to banish any trace of the divine from your lives. You don't live by God's word but set up your own new holy books in order to directly contradict God's teachings.

The Jews scream about how everyone is antisemitic, like they didn't control the world before. That's right, I said before, because now the Antichrist walks the earth. To be honest, I'm shocked you don't see the Jews worshiping the Abhorrent and the afflicted.

And that's not to even mention the Muslims! How long have we lived in fear of terrorists? And now we welcome them into our bases; we open our arms to be good Christians the way progressives have told us we have to be. We are always told that diversity is strength. Do you know the root of diversity? Divisive! Since when is divisiveness good? Coming together and everyone trying to intermingle, that isn't diversity, it's forced divisiveness, trying to create a house that is unevenly yoked between Christianity and other faiths. That reminds me of a story, the tower of Babel.

Now in the story, everyone is together and building a tower to reach heaven. The idea is that they want to be equal to God, and so God puts a stop to that by giving them all different languages. Scrambling their ability to converse. Most laymen will tell you that this is just a fable. They don't read their bible literally. But the truth is that the coming together of different tribes, each one with their own idea of heaven and God, was an abomination. We can't divvy God up into boxes. We can't pretend like everyone's faith is equally valid. The second you do, you are saying that you don't have absolute faith in Christ.

Maybe those Israelites, maybe they only wanted to build a tower to reach heaven so they could be with God. That's hubris enough; you can't reach the Father but through the Son. But even if they only wanted to be with God, there were others in that camp, other faiths that wanted to become equal to God. There's plenty of myths about the gods living on mountains, or towers, or amongst the clouds. And that's why Babel was struck down, that's why we were all punished. We were living and working with those who had no love or respect of God.

The Catholic Church is the whore of Babylon—there's no arguing with that; it's common knowledge—but they understand one thing better than anyone. That this life is a war against Satan, that there is only one way, one church under Jesus Christ, and sometimes you have fight to prove that you have the spirit worthy of heaven. The most moral thing the Catholic Church ever did, the thing that cemented them as power, that got them rewarded by God almighty, was the crusades. Destroying the enemies of God without question. That's how you survive. That's how *we* survive.

Secrets don't stay secrets on a base for long, do they? You've heard that the Abhorrent is coming, making a beeline for this base. I know you've heard the sound of the footfalls in the quietest part of the night. And I know you're scared. Hell, why wouldn't you be? I could answer that: because God will protect. But will God protect? Will God spend the energy protecting a bunch of hypocrites that make nice with heathens, who prance around with the faggots and pretend to be good people? I've seen the Abhorrent. I've watched his army of degenerate mutants and monsters marching under his feet. I've seen the death and destruction he brings. And I am telling you the only way to deflect this is to show God we mean business, that we are God's warriors, his soldiers, his crusaders.

I don't want to die. Not here, not when there are so many more lives to save. But in order to live, others must die. We must wash the sin from our hands with the blood of heathens before the Abhorrent arrives, before he brings the rapture of the fallen and we see those same heathens you want to protect changing into monsters. Kill them now, while they are human, while we still can!

God bless a righteous Christian army, and God bless America!

17.

THE BASE WAS on fire.

Ryan pushed through the smoke outside the barracks, a pistol in his hand. The congregation had exploded at Reverend King's words. Over the course of the last two months, he had been leading up to this; Ryan could see that now, that this had always been where the reverend was pushing them. But that didn't make it wrong. The reverend was a man of God, a man who took the doubt out of Ryan's mind and replaced it with an assurance that his cause was the right one. He hadn't seen Sam since their argument on the stairwell. He hoped no one had overheard what she had said, that no one knew she was an unbeliever. He could still get to her, still show her God's love.

He pushed into the barracks and ducked to avoid the smoke that was filling the building. Once they had gotten rid of the pagans and heathens, once they had cleansed the base of the unfaithful, they would need to deal with the fires. But Reverend King had promised that if they did this, the Abhorrent would change course, that the afflicted would leave them alone, that the things were drawn by the presence of non-Christian souls.

"Help!" he heard a woman's voice call. At first, he thought it was Sam, but as he got closer, he saw that it was actually his daughter's friend Rebecca and her mother, Rachel. "Ryan, thank God. Something insane is going on; we have to get out of here!"

Ryan stared at her. She was a beautiful woman, and he

had thought about her many times ever since they had arrived at the base. Every time, he had been filled with intense feelings of guilt and self-loathing. But now he understood this wasn't his fault. She was a Jew; she had been sent to test him, to corrupt him. And her daughter had befriended Sam. Was she the reason Sam was leaving the warm embrace of Jesus? Where these two really human at all, or were they simply demons sent by Hell to lead Ryan and his daughter astray? Ryan hadn't been sure if he could do this, if he could actually hurt, much less kill anyone. But seeing the full lips and dark brown eyes of Rachel and the same insidious beauty mimicked in her child, he was filled with a rage. How dare they distract him from his wife? How dare they peddle their alluring wares at good Christian families? He raised the gun and shot Rachel in the chest.

She didn't scream; she didn't have the air in her lungs to. But Rebecca screamed loud enough for both of them, trying to hold her mother up even as the light left the woman's eyes. She didn't even try to run. Ryan slid his aim to the young girl. She made him even angrier. Not only did she distract him from his wife with impure thoughts, but she was a child! He wasn't a pedophile; he was being entrapped by the insidious lasciviousness of the enemy. And not only that, she was pulling Sam away from Jesus, corrupting not just Ryan with sexual thoughts but Sam with heretical bullshit. He didn't want to kill the girl; he wanted to *hurt* her.

He stepped forward and pistol whipped the teen; the satisfying crack told him that he had done well. She collapsed and writhed on the ground, trying to reach up to force her skull to hold together despite the shattering damage it had received. Ryan watched her for a moment, savoring her pain. This was good. This was righteous. He didn't trust her to die, though. He didn't trust that when the Abhorrent came, she wouldn't mutate, shrug off the pain, and then come and find him. So he pressed his gun to the back of her head and emptied the magazine, spreading brains, skull fragments, and bits of hair-covered scalp across the barracks floor.

Rising, Ryan felt like a new man; he felt empowered. He looked down at the two women he had just killed, and something tugged at him, an anxiety that maybe he wasn't doing God's work. But he let King's words fill his mind and soul and dismissed his fears. He glanced around to make sure there were no more heathens hiding in the smoke before running out of the barracks, leaving the family of corpses to burn. He still needed to find Sam; he needed to get her out of harm's way.

He ran across the base, ejecting the spent magazine and replacing it as he moved. Everywhere he looked, there was fighting, shouting, shooting, and bloodshed. The heretics were fighting back. Ryan set his mouth in a grim smile. They could try, but they had God on their side. He heard a scream; it was unmistakable—it was Sam. Ryan turned and headed down one of the alleys between buildings, charging as fast as he could to find his daughter. The smoke made it hard to see, and the chaos around him made it hard to hear, but as he cleared a stack of boxes, he saw her.

She wasn't alone. Reverend King was restraining her with one arm around her throat. He held a syringe in his free hand, away from her so she couldn't knock it back. Ryan was confused, then his paternal instincts, frayed as they were, kicked in, and he pointed the gun at King.

"What the hell?" Ryan shouted.

"Calm down, son, calm down," King said, his voice completely lacking any sign of fear or trepidation.

"Daddy!" Sam cried, tears streaming down her face.

"What are you doing, Reverend? She isn't the enemy; she isn't a—"

"Not a what, now, brother Ryan? Not an unbeliever? Not a heathen? You know that isn't true, don't you? You know she has been talking about God, Jesus, and my church as though none of it is real, as if somehow, through trying to get people to love and accept Jesus, I'm the hateful one?" King asked, his voice strangely calm and calming to Ryan.

"Dad, he's insane! Help me!" Sam screamed.

"What's in the syringe, Reverend? What are you doing?" Ryan asked. He kept the gun up but was desperate for any explanation that would allow him to not hurt the reverend.

"Now, stop right there, Ryan. You know me, brother Ryan, you know that I am a man of God, God's chosen vessel in this time. I'm trying to save her, to make it so the Abhorrent isn't drawn to her."

"Fuck you!" Sam screamed, kicking and bucking against the arm around her neck.

"Shut up, you goddamn slut," King hissed in her ear, then loud enough for Ryan to hear: "I'm going to give her some of my blood, Ryan, my blessed blood; just like Jesus gave his blood to save us all, I'll give my blood to save her."

Ryan's gun wavered. King had said that the creatures were drawn to the unfaithful, and if that were true, then it was Sam's fault his wife was dead. It was her fault that the monster had been drawn to their car. He couldn't shoot the reverend, who was doing so much to protect Ryan's community and even now was trying to save Sam. He was a true man of God.

Ryan lowered his gun and nodded.

"What? No! Daddy!" Sam wailed.

Ryan smiled. He had killed her heathen friend, he had protected her from being corrupted further by the Jews, and now Reverend King was going to protect her from the Abhorrent. He was a good man, a good father.

King, seeing that Ryan wasn't going to interfere, pushed Sam's head aside and jammed the syringe into her neck, working the plunger with his thumb to inject the teenage girl. As soon as he had emptied the syringe, he tossed it and Sam aside, letting her fall down. He watched her writhing there, his smile growing impossibly large.

18.

KING WATCHED AS Sam began to change; it was so quick when he shared his gift with them. He'd had his eyes on the girl since arriving at the base. Everywhere he went, he chose his concubines based on human attraction—a silly thing since he was no longer human but an angelic being. But like the angelic watchers before him, he lusted for human women. He just had to remake them in his image.

"No, no, no, what the fuck is happening? Sam! Sam!" Her father, Ryan, ran towards her; he wanted to help her. Of course he did, but he couldn't. She didn't need help.

"She's changing; she's becoming divine. Like me," King offered. "The blood of the Lamb runs through my veins as God's chosen vessel, and I am sharing that gift with your daughter. It won't be the only thing I share."

"What?" Ryan looked up at him, showing those stupid trusting eyes that King could spot a mile off. "What do you mean?"

"I mean I'm going to fuck your daughter. I'm going to plant my seed deep in her waiting womb that my progeny, the progeny of heaven itself, may spread," King explained patiently. He smiled. He understood the language was crude, but the mission was holy. He was God's champion, and he, like David, Solomon, or Abraham, would spread his nation over the earth. There was no sin in choosing young and beautiful women for the task either. He would never admit it, but the bloodshed in the name of Christ and the terror in his chosen consort's parent's eyes got him harder than anything. He cherished it. He was a holy warrior; he was as high above this mortal man as God was above him.

"The hell you are," Ryan sputtered, trembling. He raised the gun again.

"That's the second time you've pointed a gun at God's chosen messenger. You really intend to spur—"

"You stay the fuck away from my daughter!" Ryan yelled. "My God, she was right—you are—"

Whatever else he was going to say was cut off as Sam lunged up and tore into his stomach with distended jaws. She was still changing, of course, but her body was already made for violence. Violence and something else.

Her face was still recognizable but only just. Her lower jaws hinged like an eel as she tore into her father with the oversized fangs and lower canines that had burst so bloodily from her gums, forcing the worthless human teeth to the ground. Her teeth, razor sharp now, had torn through his shirt and flesh easily; and even as he screamed, she pushed deeper, looking for his intestines. Her face pushed open, splitting along the seam of her skull, the flesh ripping and snapping as it made room for more teeth and a large hole with to fill with her screaming father's flesh.

King's erection swelled in the human pants he wore, straining to be released. The sight of his chosen concubine losing herself to feral hunger and eating her own father made his balls ache with a need to be emptied. His screams and the wide-eyed fear he wore on his face were better than any Viagra King had popped as a mortal man, before the angels came to him, before he was chosen. He reached down and quietly pulled off his belt and pushed down his pants. His cock, a corkscrew tangle of flesh, slick with sweat and precum, unfurled from around his leg and throbbed in the smoky hot air. The breeze tickled his cock, which trembled slightly, shaking beads of sticky thick fluid from the tip. He watched her work for a moment. He enjoyed the way her clothes—always tight enough to spark his imagination but too loose to give him a really good eyeful—bulged and split as new musculature and bones sprouted from the teenage girl.

He hoped she was not sprouting chitin—he preferred his receptacles softer than that—but in the end, all he cared about was emptying his balls into the waiting pussy of some beautiful young thing. He cleared his throat, reminding Sam that she wasn't alone to enjoy her meal. She spun, her split face knitting back together roughly, her new fangs and teeth acting like the teeth of a zipper to hold her visage together. Her eyes filled with hate, loathing, hunger; somewhere in there, he could see the girl underneath the evolution, some part of her weak human psyche trying to find the nature of her new body. She was horrified at what she had done to her father, but the flavor of his guts in her mouth was too alluring. She wanted to lash out at him, but King's eyes met hers with content domination, forcing his will on her. The Lord had gifted him with the ability to command *most* of these creatures, to force them to bend to his desires, and oh, what desires he had. It was his power that would bring the world to its knees in worship of Jesus Christ and Aiden King. She turned and tore into the screaming man again but looked back at King as if to watch for any threatening move.

He reached down and grabbed the base of his winding cock and shook it at her, flinging smegma and globs of slick precum, splattering the fluid across her blood smeared face. She winced, her lips pulling back in a snarl. But the smell hit her, and the realization of what her biology was telling her she needed hit a moment later. He could see the disgusted realization flit across her eyes; she wanted to kill him as she was killing her father. But he pushed, demanding she make herself ready, demanding that she offer herself up to him. The mental push from him was all that was needed for her basic nature of biological imperative to strike her like a ton of bricks.

ABHORRENT ACCORDS

He stepped forward and gripped the back of her torn pants with his hand, ignoring the pain of talons pushing up through his flesh. He was used to the pain that the changes brought; he relished the divinity. He never questioned the nature of the Abhorrence or the Emergence. Was it not a return to God's natural order for the man of God to wield ultimate power, for the women to prostrate themselves before him, for all to serve him? This was natural. Taking humans back to base instinct was taking them back to the Garden of Eden.

He ripped down, using his inhuman strength to pull her shredded jeans and panties down around her knees.

Then he gazed at the welcoming slit of her sex. It glistened with welcoming fluids that would ease the passage of his flesh into hers. He saw no barbs, no spines that would rip into him as he fucked her; that didn't mean they wouldn't sprout as he entered, but it wouldn't be the first time his body was forced to regrow. He could fuck her brains out and leave his throbbing cock inside her to make his escape if need be. She growled at him over her shoulder, a blend of revilement and need. Her mind was fighting him, fighting her own body, but her body was winning. She pushed her hips up, offering him a better angle for entry.

Oh, how he wanted to drop to his knees and push his tongue into her pulsating asshole. But he could feel the tread of the Abhorrent through the ground; he could hear the screams of the dying. Soon, this base would be nothing but the afflicted and their prey amongst the flattened buildings. He had no time to dally. He gave his long, misshapen shaft a last stroke and made eye contact with Ryan, a slow smile stretching across his face. He was a divine being, and it would be his beautiful smile and his ravishing of Ryan's daughter that would carry Ryan to hell.

King set the calloused head of his cock against her waiting hole and pushed in.

Sam bellowed in pain and bucked under him. The

ridges along his shaft scraped the inside of her vaginal canal. If the little slut had taken other men, he would clean her insides of their leavings. He would brook no competition inside her body. She squirmed, but he didn't relent, slamming his hips into her, working ever deeper into her body with every dominating thrust. He kept his eyes on Ryan's, maintaining eye contact, watching the bubbles of blood pop along his lips as he breathed his last. It was more than King could handle. He came hard, slamming against Sam's ass again and again as he rode his orgasms through her protesting screeches.

The best part of crafting his concubines in this new world: there was no need for cover up, no need for hush money, no need for silencing those who would not be silent. He would leave her to spawn however biology demanded she splurt out his off spring. He would be long gone, off to the next settlement to bring the good news of Jesus Christ and to find his next blissful union.

Sam stalked away from the husk of loose skin and bones that she had left over after devouring her father's entrails. She felt wretched. With the domineering presence of King gone, there was just enough of her mind left to rebel against what had happened. Not with her father; his giving her to King had blossomed into rage and disgust as her body was taken over by the affliction. She had no regrets about devouring him. The animal she was becoming and the woman she was were in alignment. Eat the men, shit them out, they were good for nothing more.

She knew what she was becoming. She understood the affliction, though she hadn't known it would be so painful, that she would be aware of her body ripping itself apart to rebuild in new, alien configurations. There was something else her biology and her dwindling humanity agreed on: ridding herself of the reverend's leavings. She considered reaching into herself and scraping out the polluted semen by hand, anything to distance herself from the preacher who had used some unearthly power to rape her, but she knew that may not work. No, better to find someplace to ride out the birth of these terrible things and then devour them. That was the only sane response to King's act—devour the unwanted newborn before they could become a threat. She had no desire to be a mother, not to these monsters, not to anything. She had to get away, get to safety.

She snapped her teeth, her entire face shuddering as the four parts of her segmented jaws came together. She needed to find safety, away from these other afflicted, away from the humans they were killing. She turned back, and her eyes, hidden in the mess of flesh and teeth that had become her face, fell on her father's prone body. There, laying on his open hand, was the gun he had waved around so ineffectively. A gun. It seemed pointless; it seemed alien. Her thoughts were muddied and swirled around her body like directionless birds flocking in confusion. But they kept coming back to the gun.

She looked down at her hands; they were claws. Several fingers had melded together, creating stronger digits for digging through the earth. She could sense that would be useful; she could dig a hole, hide in it during the pregnancy. Then her young would devour her, tear through her body so they would have the strength to hunt and live on their own. She would not eat her young, they would eat her.

She loped back to her father's body and picked up the gun, fumbling around with her new hands. No. They would not eat her. She would not eat them. She lifted the gun, pushing her smallest finger, the only one that would fit, through the trigger guard, and pushed the gun through the flaps of her face, pointing it up into the cavern of her dissolving psyche.

She was 16, and three months ago, her entire life had

stretched before her like the red carpet at a Hollywood premiere. Now there was nothing ahead but the solace of a bullet fired from the gun she had pried from her father's dead fingers.

We have no way of knowing how many settlements and outposts Aiden King is responsible for destroying. We know that he continued to show up looking and behaving entirely human after the incident at Sheppard Air Force Base. We have no idea how that's possible. Communication is so scattered and broken across the world that by the time anyone knew to look out for or beware King, the damage was already done.

From the recordings and survivor testimonies, we know that King always preceded the Abhorrent. We can trace their path through the country up until that final confrontation. Each place he went, he started small and calm; and then as more people accepted him, he would bring out the fervor and hate, transforming from a kindly reverend to a fire and brimstone iconoclast, whipping his followers into a frenzy that took too many lives. We don't know if he honestly believed he was doing God's work or if he was simply destabilizing human populations as part of symbiotic evolution of the afflicted. A scout that cleared the way for the monstrous. While his purpose is obfuscated, one thing is excessively clear: King was exceedingly capable of turning people against each other and relished doing so.

Even though so many are quick to dismiss King as "not a real Christian," that would be ignoring that similar terror was sown across the world. We saw holy men working to sway their congregations towards violence—xenophobia was our master—and for every community that came together, there were six more that were torn apart by infighting, who put together raids to steal supplies from people who looked, sounded, or prayed differently.

Many of us learned if we were religious, to hide it. We never knew who would blame the Abhorrence on our Judaism, our skin color, our sexuality; we never knew who would drive us out or try to kill us because we didn't worship a make-believe deity the way they did. Even in monotheistic communities, we saw that fundamentalists would sacrifice their more lenient counterparts, dismiss them as not true followers.

JOHN BALTISBERGER

Other than his affliction, Aiden King was no different than a hundred thousand other holy rollers who took on the mantle of savior in order to reap the rewards of power. Sometimes I wonder that the Abhorrence hasn't put a final stake in the heart of supernatural faith.

If there was some magical being who loved us, how could this happen?

But still, clergy come forward all the time to help rebuild while truly just rebuilding their congregation and base of power. People may be more skeptical than ever, but the truth is they are also more scared and more desperate for some comforting belief and community to cling to. We're all desperate for warmth in the cold post-Abhorrence reality.

Alexander Fienkolt
University of Texas, Archivist

PART 4:

FINALE

19.

MEXICO

RICO SAT IN the small room and stared at the radio. Almost a solid year, a year of death and fighting. Early in the Abhorrence, he and the others had dreams of taking the fight to the afflicted, taking back their cities. Rico himself wanted to find his son. Even if he was a monster, Rico needed to find him; he needed the closure. But of course, that was impossible. If Gil was still alive, he wasn't Gil anymore. He would be unrecognizable; he would be just another murderous, hungry monster that Rico had to put down. And that was all there had been, a year of putting down monsters and trying to find whatever the new normal was.

But now . . .

Now the radios had come back to life. It was a cause for celebration at first, especially as little surviving communities made contact with other surviving communities. It felt like the first breath of fresh air after hiding in a squalid hole for months on end. Optimism reigned as the possibility of human survival seemed to rear its head. It didn't last.

They discovered the existence of massive monsters ravaging the world, things that stood over cities and spread the disease with their every breath. The existence of giant monsters, things like Godzilla or King Kong, blew Rico's mind. How could such creatures exist? They called them *megafuana* and *kaiju*. But the fact of the matter was they were titanic monsters that were destroying cities without a thought.

The terror didn't stop there.

It started as whispered rumors between survivalist outposts. Word that things were stabilizing, that the afflicted were being pushed back. But more than that, that they had found the source of the affliction, and it was Mexico's fault. No details as to why, only that some gringo scientist had pointed his finger at his southern neighbors. No one bought it, but the idea that the world was ready to blame Mexicans sent a chill down Rico's spine; and whenever he was free, he would spend time in the little room they kept the radio and TV in, listening for any bit of news.

Tonight, he and Miguel were sitting around the radio, sipping cheap tequila they had scavenged from one of the nearby ghost towns. In most areas, humans were gone and the afflicted had either moved on or found nests. It was still dangerous; you never knew when one of those motherfuckers was going to burst out from the dilapidated buildings and charge you, but at least now they weren't *everywhere*. So little forays into neighboring towns to steal gas, food, and the occasional dirty magazine were, in their minds, well worth the risk.

He had hoped to hear news of people fighting back, maybe the government or one of the cartels taking the fight to the afflicted and clearing out the cities. That was how it happened, right? In every monster or zombie movie, humanity was pushed back to the fringe by the threat and then they banded together to take back the planet. Instead, there were whispers of something far worse, not coming together but a falling apart. The cause of the affliction, the very nature of the malady, had been traced back to narcotics that had come from Mexico. Not just from Mexico but from the Hernandez Cartel and their allies specifically.

Miguel sat back, the bottle of tequila held loose in his

fingers; from the look on his face, he was just as numb as Rico, unable to process what they were hearing. It wasn't just rumors anymore either. The voices on the radio were angry, talking about what to do and, more importantly, who to do it to. Rico reached over and flipped the radio off. The two men sat in stunned silence for several minutes before Miguel cleared his throat.

"What—"

"I don't know," Rico said, cutting off the question—it didn't matter what the question was going to be; he didn't have any answers . . . for any questions.

"It can't be true, right?" Miguel asked after another minute of silence.

"Why can't it? You saw it. We've all seen it," Rico snapped.

They had; over the course of the year, they had seen the truth of the cause. There had been girls. They had known that the Hernandez Cartel dealt in prostitution and trafficking; everyone knew. And while Rico, Miguel, and Beto had tried to remain "above the criminal element" of their hosts at first, the truth was that they all needed to let off some steam, they all needed to fuck and feel like men.

Of course, one method the Cartel used for controlling their "merchandise" was addiction. They just hadn't put two and two together to make four, even after Beto was ripped in half by an afflicted whore minutes after she was shot up to make her more . . . "compliant." No scratches, no exposure to anything—other than the heroin that had entered her veins. They had experimented after that, testing what had happened. Was it rape? Stress? Was it the drugs or her genetics? Rico had participated in the trials as well, telling himself that this was in the name of science; these girls, their families were dead, their lives were gone, but they could do something useful.

That's what he told himself when he stood over them, when he came in them. It's what he told himself when he couldn't sleep because of the things he had done.

But it became obvious quickly: the catalyst was the drugs. And now they knew it wasn't all drugs, it wasn't just heroin in general. It was the heroin and opiates that had been produced and shipped out from the Hernandez Cartel, from the group they had joined at the beginning of all of this. They were responsible.

Rico reached over and took the bottle from Miguel. He took a long swig, swallowing the awful liquor before setting it down. He glanced at the radio, wondering if he should turn it back on, try to find more information, wondering if more information would even matter. Next to the radio was his gun.

They carried their guns everywhere. In case.

In case an afflicted got in, in case some raider wanted a piece of what they had, in case, in case . . . in case. There was always a reason to be armed. Rico stared at the weapon for several minutes. A white noise filled the room as Miguel worked through the information they now had, information that was, at least in this mansion, theirs alone. Rico picked up the pistol, holding it out, feeling the weight of it, imagining that it was the weight of what he had to do. He could pretend he never heard the radio, continue to live in the relative peace and luxury that the alliance with the cartel had allowed.

Or he could not. It was their fault that his wife was dead, that his daughters were dead, that his son had become an inhuman monster. It was their fault that he had become a monster himself. How many people who had clamored at the gates for safe passage had he shot down just to keep the supplies they had from dwindling faster? How many women, no, girls had he enjoyed, knowing what he was doing was monstrous but denying his guilt through flimsy excuses? He was no better than they were. He had sucked at the tit of decadence and hedonism when they gave him the opportunity.

He couldn't erase that guilt; he couldn't change what he had done. He looked up at Miguel, meeting the larger man's eyes.

"We go now, maybe we can get out of here before they realize . . . " Miguel whispered.

Rico shook his head. "No."

"No?"

"No," Rico repeated. "No, we owe the world, I owe my family more than that," he said, his voice shaking. He stood. "I'm going to kill them."

"Rico, man, we can't . . . "

"You heard the fucking radio, Miguel. You telling me you're good with this? You telling me you're okay with what they did? What *we* did?" Rico snarled, trying to keep his voice down.

Miguel stared at Rico for a long time. The man was a loyal friend, strong, fast, but he had never been a leader, happy to let other people do the thinking for him. Finally, Miguel lowered his eyes and shook his head. "No."

"Me either. We make this right. Right now, right here." Rico popped the magazine out of the pistol and checked the ammo before slamming it back in place. "We do this tonight."

20.

PARKER, COLORADO

DENVER WAS HIT hard by the Emergence, but there were plenty of fortifiable compounds and prepper stashes in Colorado, so several pockets of human settlements existed. In Parker, for example, the residents had set up and fortified Legend High School. From there, they went on forays, setting up teams who would clear the area of Afflicted, burn them, and then set up a new perimeter. In this way, the Legend High School settlement slowly grew and became self-sufficient—one of the first to do so in the post-Abhorrence United States.

Aiden King stared up at the gates, a grim smile on his face. Finally, he thought, finally there was a sizable and seizable community. He raised his hand as he approached, a friendly hello, showing whoever was on the other side—an armed guard, no doubt—that he did not bear the mark of the beast. King's eyes moved over the gate; it wouldn't keep the afflicted out, but it had been a week of travel, and he hadn't seen but a few of the afflicted on his trek here. This settlement was more efficient than others, more bloodthirsty. It would be easy to pull them apart, to bring the true followers of Christ forward to wash away the unbelievers as they had the afflicted.

"Stop there," a voice called out, crackling over a speaker mounted near the gates. "The gates are electrified, and we have several guns trained on you." The voice sounded bored, as though interrogating wandering preachers was old hat for him.

"I'm stopped," King said, raising his other arm in mock surrender. "Ain't gotta ask me twice, friend."

"How many of you are there?" the voice asked.

"How many? Well so far as I know"—*Legion, we are legion*—"I'm all by my lonesome." He smiled through the indignity.

"Just you?" Incredulity filled the voice. "Where are you coming from?"

Now that radios were starting to work again, King knew he had to be a bit more careful; after all, who knew what got out during his last revelry? It wouldn't do to be caught unawares by paranoid gunmen. "I've been searching for survivors for weeks. I was in Texas, but . . . you know what happened there, I assume." King lowered his eyes and put a hand over his heart as if mourning the loss of the great state. "Been on the run ever since."

There was a long silence as whoever was watching him, either through the fence or through the small CCTV camera King saw, considered his words. He imagined they were wondering why his clothes looked so nice, why he looked so healthy.

"Any scratches?" the voice suddenly asked. "Have you ingested or injected any form of opiate, heroin, morphine, fentanyl, or any other form of pain killer in the last week?"

Scratches, King understood, but not the other part. "Uh, no, I'm not a junkie; I'm a man of God, a preacher. Reverend Aiden King. Why would you—"

"Standard question; the affliction spreads through the use of painkillers and opiate narcotics," the voice snapped, taking King aback.

Was that true? King paused, his watery blue eyes staring unblinking at the gate. It wouldn't make a difference to him, not really. He had seen that junkies were the first to change, but maybe his own use of Valium had set off his own gift? No, that was ludicrous; he was chosen by God and to command the marked. If junkies were the first to change, it was because they engaged in acts that God despised, it was because they gave themselves to the beast. The junkies were whores and faggots. Rapists, murderers, and thieves. He had had no patience for them when they were in their human guise, and now as marked afflicted, their use was utilitarian. He spread the word of God and afflicted those he wanted to serve him directly—carnally or as protection.

"No," King finally said softly. "No scratches, no drugs."

He waited in awkward silence, wondering if they would open the door or leave him out there. Eventually, though, the gate swung open and he was greeted by the sight of five armed guards in body armor—better equipped here than anywhere else. He slowly lowered his arms to his side.

"Well, praise God!" King said, stepping forward, only to be brought up short by one of the guards.

"Here's the deal, dude. You can come in, restock, resupply; hell, if you can carry your weight in work and labor, you can even stay. But there's none of that religious stuff, not publicly."

"What?" King bristled.

"We're a . . . freedom from religion sort of community. If you want to worship Jesus in the privacy of your own lodging, that's fine. But we don't allow for public preaching."

"Are you saying that there are no Christians here?" King asked. Everywhere he went, the Christians were falling short of their duty of proselytizing, of spreading the good word, but to find there was a huge settlement where Christianity was banned was insane.

"Not at all. I'm saying they worship and pray in the privacy of their own homes. We've had issues with holy men before. Too much division, too much danger and . . . and abuse. So we as a community don't allow for it. Now, agree to that and we can—"

"Agree to that? Agree to what? Hide my love of Jesus?

Sit back and watch sinners frolic and deny the divinity of the Lord? You have more of a settlement here than any other I've seen, and you just sit around ignoring the one who has given you so much?" King knew that he should calm down, that if he just played ball, he could find the Christian community, get them to rise up, to take over the settlement. But it would be slow; it would be so much slower if he had to do it all in secret.

His goal was to save souls, save souls and find those who would serve and service him. And if he took too long, the Beast would catch up before he had a chance to sow the seeds (both of salvation and his own). Then it was all for naught. He might be able to find a new concubine, a new Hagar or Keturah, before the place was destroyed, but his opportunity to set the lost on a path of righteousness would be denied.

"We don't deny shit. But organized religion has been an excuse to hurt people too long. We won't forbid people from practicing their faith, but no . . . we aren't going to allow it to damage our community and safety either." There were a few nods among the guards as they agreed.

King was taken aback. And furious. He could feel himself shaking with a rage he hadn't felt since he had gone toe-to-toe with that rabbi. Here he was again, among Christ-deniers. His smile stretched as he fought to retain composure. "Shouldn't it be up to the people? Community is important, especially for Christians; faith grows when—"

"Stop. We aren't interested. Those are the rules."

"Not interested?" King spat. "Not interested in saving your soul? This progressive bullshit where everyone is equal is why we're in the end times! It's why the antichrist has risen." He was getting louder, getting redder, fury enveloping him. "You don't want to offend anyone, so you say happy holidays and pretend the Muslims and Jews and fucking Satanists are your equal, and then you offend the one who died for your fucking sins?" He could feel the divine surfacing, his flesh molding and morphing. He could feel it, and by the way the guards were raising their weapons, they could see it too.

"Afflicted!" one of them cried, firing off a shot.

King took the bullet in the shoulder. He had been shot before, but usually when he was fully embraced in the divine form of angels; as a human, it hurt so much worse. He darted forward before any of the others could fire and tore into the first guard with a hand that was swiftly forming into a barbed and bony blade. He knew no fear as he slipped the bladed limb under the collar of the vest the man wore and ripped out his ribcage through the side. He was God's chosen, an angel walking the earth; he was second only to Jesus in his divinity. And he would raze this Gomorrah himself.

King shook the remains of the man's torso off his arm and turned to kill the next guard, but rather than the panicked running and screaming he was used to, the soldiers were just backing away calmly, lifting their guns and firing. Each bullet tore a furrow of pain and blood into King as his body swelled to monstrous proportions, flesh bubbling like caramel left too long in the pot.

For every hit they landed on him, his bulk swelled and he lost a bit more humanity. King raged, losing himself to the surfacing divinity within as he charged the guards, bladed limbs scything back and forth, catching one of the slower guards across the stomach and easily slicing him in half. His upper torso soared through the air and landed on the fence, where the current of the electrified metal began cooking what was left of the man.

Still the three surviving guards didn't lose their nerve. These were men and women who had survived the Emergence, who had fought day and night for close to a year against the nightmares of the affliction. And while they had never seen someone go from human to afflicted so quickly, they had lost the initial instinct of panic, replaced it with a cold and hateful spite that kept them firing again and again.

ABHORRENT ACCORDS

King took a step forward, intent on killing the three guards ahead of him, but the world was swimming, growing dimmer. This had never happened before. What new feeling of weakness was this? Every instinct in his swollen, grotesque form screamed at him to turn and run, to flee the danger. But King's will remained human iron-clad. The vestigial part of him that was the Reverend Aiden King refused to believe he could die. He was the chosen; he was the might of God on Earth to pave the way for the apocalypse and Jesus Christ's return.

He fell to one knee, the air he pulled into his lungs escaping from him through the holes that bullets had punched in his body. He couldn't breathe; he couldn't feel his hands. He glared at the guards—how dare they seek to harm the harbinger of God, the vanguard of the Abhorrent. His lips peeled back from gums that were lined in ragged bone. Tendrils of flesh whipped over his back, snapping towards the defiant apostates that were filling his form with holes. He couldn't reach them. He collapsed onto his hands, which gave out, forcing him onto his belly like some disgusting worm or serpent. He looked at them, his eyes unable to focus, unable to really see anymore.

"Jayshu wi vruck ur skulls apar," he slurred, "praish he—"

His final hymn was silenced as a young woman, one whom he would have loved to get to know better through affliction and fucking, lifted her rifle and blew his fucking skull to pieces.

The body twitched on the ground for a minute, the last of its synapses firing erratically before it fell still. Christina Rangel stared at the body, not lowering her rifle until the last bit of movement stopped. She slowly let the rifle fall and dangle from the shoulder strap, and shook her head. Two dead. It wasn't too terrible a loss from a numeric point of view, but these two . . . Eddy Lee and Robbie Darko, they were friends. They had been friends. Now they were meat. They would be incinerated alongside the body of the monster that had killed them. She sighed, closing her eyes against the pain of more loss, and moved to Eddy's corpse and rolled him over to get to the walkie-talkie he kept on his belt.

Clicking it over, she spoke quickly. "This is Rangel over at the South East gate. Two down, but get on the radio, let people know we have a new kind of afflicted. Looks like they can emulate humans and change faster. Over."

There was a long pause while Zach Ashford, captain of their little guard outfit, digested that information. "Come again? Over," he finally said.

"He changed; the afflicted changed so quickly. One minute he was—" She paused, taking in a juddering breath. "Look, just send a jeep for the bodies and gear. I'll explain when I get back to HQ." She looked over the corpses one last time. All she could do was pray that this would be the last time that she had to burn the bodies of the people she cared about, but in her heart, she knew that the cycle of violence and death would never cease.

21.

PARKER, COLORADO

ONE MONTH, almost to the day, since Aiden King was executed outside the gates of the Parker, Colorado settlement, the earth shook with terrible finality. Terror and death had stalked the United States for near 12 months and had shown no signs of stopping. The Abhorrent had been nuked, and while the heat of the blast had blistered the creature's hide, and certainly killed off many of the afflicted that cavorted under its massive claws, the beast was otherwise undaunted. Indeed, attacking it, even with the full might of the United States' nuclear arsenal, only seemed to spur it on to greater heights of destructive violence.

Few knew of the other kaiju that stalked across the country. The Abhorrent had emerged before the complete collapse of telecommunications; the nameless possum had only come after, the only witnesses to its rage silenced forever by mutation or death.

But now the ground vibrated with the footfalls of titans coming together.

The Abhorrent knew that something was wrong, something strange and terrible, something dangerous. It was not naturally a predator; it had been born a thing that ate plants and hid from danger, but that was a lifetime ago. Now it knew no danger; its hunger was not sated by plants but by the myriad little creatures that scattered under its footsteps.

Its eyesight was terrible, especially above the water, but it could see the towering shape that lumbered across the mountains towards it. At last, a true meal, enough meat to sate its raging and voracious hunger. It lumbered forward, crushing the electric fence that had kept the community safe for so long and allowing the flood of afflicted through. They poured like a tsunami across the city, riding the pink miasmic tide towards their human prey.

For their part, the humans knew the Abhorrent was on its way. They had stayed on the radio, listening to reports, following its trajectory as it approached the southeast border of their sanctuary. They had headed to the northwest, intent on fleeing, getting out of its way. They had not known about the other titanic monstrosity that now crested the Rocky Mountains. They were not ready as the gate folded under its claws and allowed its own horde access to the humans within.

Parker, Colorado, for all of its wealth of unity and firepower, was no different than any town or city that met with the kaiju of the Abhorrence. The people died in droves. Families who had lasted a year with no painkillers, who had escaped the cities and come together as a community to survive, fell apart at the indifferent assault from the Abhorrent. Their stoicism and training were not rewarded with mercy, or even a quick death. The pink fog that bellowed from titanic jaws seeped into the pores and orifices of the citizens, taking a hold of their physiology and forever twisting it to new and nightmarish forms.

A woman cried for her children even as she ripped them apart, peeling back soft flesh to find the delicate flavors of the spleen inside.

A grandfather cried as he leveled the shotgun first at his wife and then turned it on himself, too old, too tired, to fight any longer.

Those unchanged lived only to see the evolution of their neighbors into the very monsters they had been fighting for so long. Christina Rangel stood on the edge of the radio tower staring down at the chaos. She had gone up there to report back to the ground what was happening, to coordinate the evacuation. She had been the first to see the mammalian behemoth and the first to see the coming Abhorrent. They were so much bigger than she could have ever imagined. The thing from the west that looked so much like a possum whipped its tail at the Abhorrent, the bellowing thunder crack shaking the tower Rangel stood on like it was made of popsicle sticks. The warning hiss that the creature issued nearly blew her off her perch, and as the pink mist that accompanied the action blew past her, she felt the terrible twisting in her gut, she felt her bones stretching at the call of mutation.

She knew what was happening. She could feel the affliction coursing through her body. It demanded she climb down the tower and tear into the meat on offer there. She needed it. She needed food, shelter . . . and something else. But she wouldn't allow that; she was still human enough to understand what was happening. Without a second thought, Christina Rangel threw herself off the side of the tower, opening her arms to embrace the coming earth.

She never reached it. With a snap of its jaws, the Abhorrent snatched her out of the air, crushing her bones and organs to paste that sluiced down its gullet. The Abhorrent swallowed and let out its own enraged roar, rising to its hind legs to appear even bigger, towering over the mayhem of Parker Colorado.

The possum met the Abhorrent's challenge, and the two creatures crashed into each other, claws tearing great chunks out of each other's hide. Where nuclear arms and rocket fire had done nothing but irritate the beast, razor talons did the real work. Bioluminescent blood poured from wounds the size of buses, raining down glowing sanguine fluids to the world below, drowning those afflicted who were too slow to flee the deluge.

Neither creature could back down, the hunger and hatred driving them into each other's claws, a primal force more powerful than even self-preservation. The possum had greater agility, its claws and needle-sharp teeth peeling back layers of flesh with each swipe. But the Abhorrent was so much bigger, so much angrier, and the slime that covered it protected it from much of the harm.

The two beasts writhed in the dirt as each sought to gain dominance over the other, spurred on by hateful instincts that screamed in their distorted brains that the only survival was survival of domination. They could not back down; they would not cede territory to the other.

The possum screamed an earth-shattering cry as the Abhorrent bit into its throat, crushing its windpipe. In its panic, it punched at the Abhorrent, frenzied blows that pulped the flesh and bone of the mighty beast. Finally, the possum's curled fist found purchase in the Abhorrent's eyes, punching through the flesh and digging into the skull beneath.

The Abhorrent could heal from any wound it survived, regrowing limbs, growing stronger to fight, but even it couldn't live through the terrible trauma done to its cranial meat. The Abhorrent spasmed, its jaws working, clamping shut, masticating the possum's throat and skull, forcing meat and gore to push its way up and out of the creature's throat, nose, and eyes.

The two giants fell, gods that sacrificed themselves on the altar of vicious instinct. Their disciples, the millions of afflicted, both human and animal, fell onto the flesh of their dead deities. They paid homage with tooth and nail, glorifying the instinct as they sought food and fucked in the folds of the glowing flesh of abhorrence.

INTERVIEW WITH FREDERICO SANCHEZ

ASSISTED WITH TRANSLATION BY ISIS VALENCIA

FREDERICO SANCHEZ: I once said that all of our talk about the cartels was just lip service. I don't think any of us that have survived can ever forgive that lip service and apathy, not now.

When we first discovered that it was drugs that was causing the changes, when that bit of news came through, it made everything harder. We banded together—federales, gangsters, everyone. We knew it was us Mexicans against the creatures. But once we discovered it was because of the drugs, drugs that came out of Mexico, fuck, man. It tore us apart. The world blamed us; we were the new villains. Of course, America led the charge, just like Americans had to Muslims civilians after their World Trade

Center attack, just like Americans had when they figured out that Covid had come out of China. The difference was Mexico was to blame and that this wasn't just citizens, this was the entire fucking country.

So, yeah, the world hated us, and we pressed that hate down towards the drug dealers and cartels. It was their fault, right? They spread the poison around. Worldwide distribution meant that there was hardly a place in the world that wasn't touched, wasn't ruined, because of the greed of wicked men.

ALEXANDER FIENKOLT: How did the anti-Mexican rhetoric effect you and your efforts to combat the Abhorrence? Even knowing that the Abhorrence wasn't limited to the opiates coming out of Mexico, it did seem to be the first step in tainting the world's morphine and fentanyl supplies.

SANCHEZ: Terribly. Not at first, obviously. I mean by the time scientists traced the cultures and tainted drugs back to Cartel owned labs and crops . . . by then, the communication infrastructure was almost gone. At first, we laughed, you know. Oh the gringos are shit-talking and blaming Mexicans? Of course they are; that's what they do. Of course, once the truth got here, then it got ugly. Everyone always talks about how bad the Abhorrence messed up the United States, how bad it was there. But shit was real bad here. We didn't have the giant monsters like the one that popped up in Russia, or Iran, or the couple that ravaged America. But Mexico wasn't in good shape.

FIENKOLT: No one was. No one is.

SANCHEZ: Right, there isn't a place that isn't destroyed. But my point is that people, other countries, were all treating Mexico as though we had done this on purpose, as a country. It wasn't the cartels who has poisoned the world and the water and set loose this terrible thing. It was Mexico; it was Mexicans. When we found out, we weren't better. We turned on the gangsters as quickly as the world turned on us. The problem, of course, is that we had teamed up with them. We had made friends; we had saved each other . . . We owed the bastards our lives.

FIENKOLT: So it was hard to turn on them?

SANCHEZ: No, I wish it had been. I have nightmares about those days. Fighting monsters is one thing, even monsters that used to be your friends. But this was humans. We were fighting humans. What made it hard is that they had the guns. They had ammo. More so than anything we could get from the police stations and federal armories. I think we all expected the cartels to step up and fill the void that the government left. Maybe we optimistically thought that they would even be better. Corrupt, yes, but the shared experience of fighting together, dying together would change their leadership to be more humane. Now instead, we were fighting a coup against the people we had relied on to keep us alive.

FIENKOLT: Why fight them, though? I understand it was their doing, but it wasn't on purpose, and it seems counterproductive to . . .

SANCHEZ: To what, man? To bite the

hand that feeds you poisoned food? We were angry; we were so angry. I still am angry. But more than that, we were afraid. We didn't have a lot of communication, but we could still catch bits and scraps.

FIENKOLT: The nukes.

SANCHEZ: The nukes. Can you imagine how afraid we were? And we thought, I don't know what we thought. We hoped that us rising against the cartels would make it so the world could see we weren't complicit, that we didn't unleash this terror on them, that we, too, were hurting and broken. We thought that if we did this, we could avoid the nukes. Or failing that, we hoped to take our own pound of flesh out of them for what they had cost us.

FIENKOLT: So you wanted to make them pay for the dead, the people killed during the Abhorrence?

SANCHEZ: I wanted to make them pay for costing us our humanity. The Abhorrence changed so many, obviously, it stole their humanity in a way you could see. But what about me and those like me? People who had to kill their fathers or children. People who were unchanged on the outside but who became monsters as surely as any of the afflicted. That is what I wanted to make them pay for. Innocence lost, the ability to sleep without seeing the nightmares of my sweet son changing into something else, something dangerous and hungry for his sisters. I can't speak for anyone else, but I wanted blood; I wanted someone to blame.

FIENKOLT: And doing that, did it make you better? Did it ease any of that pain?

SANCHEZ: <laughing> Of course not; it did nothing for me. I killed men because I thought I should, because I was angry and needed to. A biological imperative just like the afflicted. I am no better. In the end, the nukes fell. In the end, the cartels may have been to blame, but everyone who was compliant and paid lip service was no better; our hands are no cleaner.

FIENKOLT: You blame yourself?

ABHORRENT ACCORDS

SANCHEZ: You don't? Listen, if you don't blame yourself, then you are either ignorant or delusional. You didn't do everything in your power to stop the drugs, to stop people's madness. You slept, you rested easy on those things that were easy, and you decided that anything that was too hard was "out of your control." We all did; we all owe our piece of the puzzle to the Abhorrence.

FIENKOLT: So what do we do about that?

SANCHEZ: I've done what I can. I killed afflicted, looters, corrupt soldiers, and human monsters seeking to profit from all the terror. I've killed people I thought might be becoming afflicted only to find out they were diagnosed with epilepsy, and I've killed gangsters. So many gangsters. There's almost no one left to kill.

FIENKOLT: Almost?

<Sanchez looks at me like he envies me. It's a haunted expression I've seen so many times in the last year. He's tired. But so am I. Maybe that

will make me complicit, but the pain I see in his eyes is something I don't feel equipped to help. I'll rest on this, sleep on this hurt that is out of my control.>

SANCHEZ: I've already told you who I blame.

FINAL THOUGHTS

EVERYONE WANTED TO return to normal after the Fall of the Abhorrent kaiju. Obviously, we did what we could to eradicate the afflicted, and with the fall of pharmaceuticals and the health care structure, there were fewer and fewer new cases of affliction. Normalcy was a dream that we fooled ourselves into believing was achievable.

Republican Senator Max Booth III led that charge. He believed that by helping reestablish American politics, he would be an easy choice for president. And despite his intentions, he did a lot of good. He helped rebuild the telecommunications industry, even if it was just so that he could campaign. Really, the physical infrastructure for our country was already in place, barring what was destroyed by the kaiju and their fight. What was missing were the people, little vital bits of information that had been stored in the brains of those who were killed or became afflicted. We just had to rebuild and place the right people in the right places until the systems could be turned on again.

Booth led those talks that led to the nuclear bombs being dropped over Mexico, in places where the afflicted were thickest—the nests, he called them. Countries with nuclear capabilities had struck out against the kaiju to little effect, but this was the first and thankfully last time that such terrible firepower was aimed at afflicted. How effective these bombs were in killing off the afflicted and their hives, I doubt we'll ever really know, especially now that those cities are practically uninhabitable.

Just like central Colorado—while there's no nuclear fallout, the corpses of the kaiju who fell there, and those who emerged and died in other parts of the world, continue to exert their mutating presence upon the surrounding area, leaving entire states and territories shrouded in the terrible pink mist that has become synonymous with affliction. We've walled off those areas, and we've convinced ourselves we've seen the last of them, though we know that's unlikely true either. Between the bombs and the monsters, we're left with a staggering amount of the planet we can no longer inhabit.

We didn't repeat similar bombings in other nests in other countries; it seemed, and still seems, to have been a move more powered by spite than anything. But I'm not sure we could have avoided the bombs even without his fear-mongering. The world was terrified, and more than that, as Sanchez said, the world was angry. So Mexico became a scapegoat.

As for Senator Booth, his dreams of becoming president and, in his words, "making America the power that Reagan had built" were short lived. His ties to big pharmaceutical companies had been prior knowledge, but he should have known that his part in deregulating oversight and paving the way for their use of the tainted opioids would be dug up by his opposition. He was just another hate-monger, like Aiden King. He may not have been afflicted, but his goals were the same: take power at the expense of human life and humanity. He was killed by an angry mob outside his house less than 24 hours after the story broke. Of course, his death hit off a new wave of political strife, as an equal number of people celebrated his death as called him a martyr. We had achieved some sense of the normalcy that we had before the Emergence.

I can't pretend that I didn't crave a return to the world we had before the Abhorrence; who wouldn't? But I keep thinking about how, in the end, it was that very world that caused the Abhorrence to happen, how it was filled with inequality, racial tension, bigotry, and government corruption. We live in a nightmare where the afflicted still crawl from the cracks in facades to spread panic and death, where we always have to be afraid of new monsters emerging from the places we once ignored.

Looking back on everything that has happened, we have tried to paint a picture of the entire Abhorrent event; we've written what we could, trying to piece together how it all went so very wrong. The truth is that while I've done so much work to understand the past, I have to admit it's an effort to avoid looking into the future. Who are we as a species? How will we overcome what's happened?

History is written by the victors, but the future is written by the survivors. I, for one, don't know that we have survived; I don't know that there is a future to write.

Alexander Fienkolt
University of Texas, Archivist

ACKNOWLEDGEMENTS

This book, the final of the Abhorrent Trilogy... it wouldn't exist without a few key people, my mom, Jackie Gulledge, for buying me Godzilla vs. Mechagodzilla 2 on VHS, (which I wore the tape out of). My uncle Jay Gulledge for showing me Godzilla vs. Biollante while I was in Boston.

I have to give my love to Lucas Mangum, Max and Lori Booth, Charles Bernard, Christine Morgan, Maxwell Bauman, Kevin Welch, John "Rudie" Overton, Shane McKenzie and a whole slew of people who keep me sane when everything seems hopeless.

I also want to thank Lisa Tone, Edward Lee, Nat Whiston, and Mike Rankin, for always encouraging me and reminding me that I should keep putting pen to paper.

ABOUT THE AUTHOR

John Baltisberger is an award-winning author of speculative and genre fiction that often focuses on Jewish Elements. Through his writing, he has explored themes of mysticism, faith, sin, and personal responsibility. Known for his bizarre blend of Jewish mysticism and splatter, his work has spanned extreme horror, urban fantasy, science fiction, cosmic horror, epic verse, and non-fiction. He is the Creative Director at Madness Heart Games and has worked on such games as Odd Gobs, Splatter League, Mork Borg, Liminal_, Vast Grimm, and more. He can be found at http://linktr.ee/kaijupoet.

MORE FROM JOHN BALTISBERGER

Abhorrent Siren
Abhorrent Accords
Blood & Mud
All I Want is to Take Shrooms & Listen to the Color of Nazi Screams
Unclean Verses
Whispers of the Dead Saint
War of Dictates
Jungles of Habbiel
Children of the Gods
No Guilt of Bloodshed
The Hillels Have Eyes
Treif Magic
Son of the Righ Hand
Sheyd of Gray

ALSO, FROM ST ROOSTER BOOKS

To Be One with You: An Anthology of Parasitic Horror
Kids of the Black Hole; A Punksploitation Anthology
*The Blind Dead Ride Out of Hell; A Literary Tribute to
the Amando de Ossorio Films*
A New Life by Paul Lubaczewski
The God Provides by Thomas R Clark
3 Hits from the Holler by Paul Lubaczewski
Let the World Drown: An Anthology of Sea Horror
Souls in a Blender by Lamont A Turner
Hungry Cosmos by Reed Alexander
Black Friday: An Elder's Keep Collection by Jeffery X Martin
Short Stories About You by Jeffery X Martin
I Never Eat . . . Cheesesteak by Paul Lubaczewski
Hunting Witches by Jeffery X Martin
Saint's Blood by Ryan C Bradley
As the Night Devours Us by Villimey Mist
Parham's Field by Jeffery X Martin
SummerHome by Thomas R Clark
The Ridge by Jeffery X Martin
*Through the Mist and the Madness: An Analytical
Thesis on the First Three Metallica Albums* by Jerome
Reuter
Like a Ton of Bricks by Paul Lubaczewski
The Flock by Jeffery X Martin
A Prayer from the Dead by Thomas R Clark
Wax Figures by Aaron Weese
*Razor Blade in the Fun-Size Candy: A Horror Comedy
Anthology*
Bleeding Out in the Rain by Lamont A Turner
Brooklyn Hardcore by Eddie MacNamara
Even More Monsters by Paul Kane
*Electric Funeral: Black Sabbath and the Cultural
Landscape 1970-1975* by Jerome Reuter